NEVER SLEEP

THE FIRST CHRONICLE OF A LADY DETECTIVE

K.B. OWEN

Never Sleep
the personal chronicle of a lady detective

Copyright © 2015 Kathleen Belin Owen

Cover design by Melinda VanLone, BookCoverCorner.com

ISBN-13: 978-0-9974674-8-2

CHAPTER 1

November 1885

Rose Glen, Massachusetts

I hadn't seen Frank Wynch in nearly three years, but not much about him had changed. Yes, his hairline had receded and his jaw was shadowed with graying stubble, but he still carried his tall, lanky frame with the vigor I remembered, and his sharp hazel eyes missed little.

It was as if the years had dropped away for me and my estranged husband. But I couldn't allow myself to forget what drove us apart. This was an assignment, nothing more.

The windy train platform had me buttoning my travel cloak close to my neck and tucking blonde strands of hair back in their pins.

Frank hefted my case. "What have you got in here, a set of encyclopedias?"

I smiled. "Your telegram said I'm to be Mr. Comstock's personal assistant. One would assume the position is of some duration." My eyes conveyed the unspoken inquiry: *what will I really be doing?* A thrill of anticipation prickled my spine. It had been a long time since I'd worked with my Pinkerton husband.

As we threaded our way through the crush of disembarking passengers, he leaned closer. "It will appear to the rest of the household that you are Miss Hamilton, employed to take dictation for Henry Altree Comstock and catalogue his notes as he prepares his family's memoirs. I couldn't put more in the telegram, but I knew you would catch on that I really need you for undercover work. Remember, no one is to know we are married, not even Comstock. It's simpler that way."

I nodded. Back in the old days, we had often employed such a pretense. Under those circumstances I used my maiden name, Penelope Hamilton.

Frank regarded me warmly. "It's good to see you, Pen. You look as lovely as ever."

I suppressed a snort. We both knew my tall, angular figure did not conform to the current beauty standard. Petite and curvaceous I was not. Still, I felt a flush bloom along my cheeks. Perhaps it was the wind.

He hesitated. "I wasn't sure you'd come."

I hadn't been sure myself. When his telegram had arrived several days ago, it had nearly joined the dead mouse in the dustbin. But there was no denying that I missed helping with Frank's cases. Running a boarding house and giving lessons in chinapainting to blue-blood brats helped put food on the table, but did little for my sense of adventure.

Besides, the successful completion of this assignment might convince William Pinkerton at the Chicago office back home to hire me as an operative. That would make me one of only a handful of lady detectives in the entire agency. I had to make sure Frank didn't take all of the credit, of course. In previous cases, my contribution was treated as "unofficial." Not this time.

He looked at me expectantly.

I had no intention of straying into sentimental territory. "Well, here I am," I said briskly. "Let's find a quiet table in the station's dining room, and you can tell me more about my assignment." I gave him a stern look. "For which I expect to be properly credited in your reports."

Frank smiled. "Of course, dear."

~

With only a few patrons lingering over their meals at this hour, we were able to secure a corner table to ourselves.

"You grew up in Boston," Frank began, when the waitress left with our order. "How much do you know about the Comstocks?"

"I only know them by reputation. Our families move in different circles." Thankfully. It would not do for word to reach Mother's ears that her only daughter was engaged as a private secretary. She still had not recovered from my elopement seven years ago. "The Comstocks are wealthy and respected and have lived in Rose Glen for as long as I can remember. Their textile mill employs nearly the entire town."

Frank nodded. "They also built"—he ticked off the list on his fingers—"the workers' cottages, the town's school, the library, the train depot, the park, and even one of the churches."

"They have always been known for their philanthropy," I agreed.

"Not just philanthropy," Frank said. "The Comstocks are an ambitious lot. To attract more wealthy families to summer in the area, they recently finished renovating the river dock to accommodate more water traffic and built a riverfront banquet hall for their daughter's cotillion. Which takes place this week."

I raised an eyebrow. We should be well-compensated for solving this case. Perhaps even a bonus. Heaven knows I could use the money.

"Henry Altree Comstock is responsible for the family's recent influx of wealth," Frank went on. "He'd been in the munitions business—and was making quite a name for himself in that industry—but then his father died. When H.A. took over the mill, it was sadly outdated. Townsfolk feared it would be sold to a competitor and relocated. But he turned things around, modernizing the equipment and manufacturing processes. That was fifteen years ago. Now it's thriving." He frowned. "Until recently, that is."

The waitress returned with our food. Once she was gone, I leaned forward. "Tell me what's happened."

"First read the report I'm sending to the agency." He passed over an envelope.

I pulled out the sheets with the familiar Pinkerton logo in the header, a watchful eye surrounded by the words *We Never Sleep*. I looked up in surprise. "Wherever did you find a typewriter and carbon sheets?" Rose Glen wasn't exactly a metropolis.

"Mr. Comstock's office is well-equipped," Frank answered, blowing upon a spoonful of chowder.

The report was thorough, listing the dates and approximate times of the three sabotage attacks, the extent of the damage, witnesses, interviews, and so on. Each of the incidents had taken place last week, within days of each other. The first was a fire set in the cutting room. Although cotton scraps are highly combustible and the result could have been disastrous, the fire was discovered and quickly extinguished with Comstock Industries' state-of-the-art fire suppression equipment. The next afternoon, wrenches were found jammed in the machinery of the mill's newest power loom. The damage was considerable. According to the report, the mill's head machinist, a man named Simon Dwyer, was still trying to repair it.

But the worst incident of all happened two mornings later. A bomb had been rigged to explode in Comstock's office upon opening his door. Comstock had been called out of town the night before and was spared, but it was a near miss for his only son Gerard, who was there to tend to administrative matters in his father's absence. He suffered cuts to his face and arms, though nothing worse.

His errand boy was not as lucky, however. The youth had apparently gone into the office ahead of Gerard. With that death, Comstock had given up on the local police and engaged the Pinkerton Agency.

I looked up from the report. "This looks to be the work of an insider, yet you state here that it could not be a disgruntled worker. Why not?"

"The mill girls *have* been airing their grievances—there was even union talk," Frank said. "But those issues were resolved several weeks ago. Comstock met with them personally and agreed to several of their demands: ten-hour days, a longer meal break, and no children hired under fifteen years of age. He didn't give them the wage increase they wanted, but they seemed satisfied with the other concessions. Also, the first two incidents occurred at the same time of day—the noon break. All of the girls were accounted for."

"What about the third incident?" I asked.

Frank's lip curled in a patronizing smile. "I highly doubt any of the girls is clever enough to devise an explosive. They have only rudimentary book learning." He tapped the sheet. "If you look further down the page, you'll find your insider. The man was careless enough to lose his tie clasp at the scene."

As I riffled through the pages, Frank dropped his voice. "Our biggest impediment to the investigation is Comstock himself. He refuses to entertain the idea of his best friend and chief executive officer being the culprit. Even though Comstock was the one who gave the man that tie clasp and recognized it immediately."

I wasn't paying much attention to Frank. I'd found the name at the bottom of the report.

Suspect: Leonard Frasier.

I swallowed. I had almost married Leonard Frasier, years ago.

My assignment just got more complicated.

I let out a quiet breath as I tried to slow the pounding in my chest. If Frank learned of my former relationship with his prime suspect—a man who would recognize me on sight—I would be promptly bundled onto the next train back to Chicago. I couldn't lose this assignment.

I steadied myself and met Frank's eye. "What's his motive?"

"Comstock recently made a will leaving the mill and shipping line to Frasier and the rest of the family's holdings to his son," he said, setting aside his empty bowl.

"So Comstock's own son won't take over the mill in the event of his father's death?" I asked incredulously. "Why?"

Frank shrugged. "It was all I could do to learn the provisions of the new will. I had to go behind Comstock's back to do it. He's a very private—and stubborn—client. He refuses to believe his friend could be behind this. He suspects Broadhurst."

"Broadhurst?" I repeated.

"Michael Broadhurst. Comstock's biggest competitor."

"A competitor would make more sense," I said. "After all, if Frasier wanted the mill, why would he destroy it?"

"Obviously, Frasier's trying to throw off suspicion," Frank said tersely. "He's counting on us blaming Broadhurst. But I'm on to him. Besides, none of the damage was irreparable."

As dearly as I hoped Frank was wrong, there was no denying the possibility. Leonard could have changed from the highly principled man I once knew. Ten years is a long time.

I sighed. "How do we proceed?"

CHAPTER 2

*M*rs. Koch, the Comstock family's housekeeper, led the way to my room with barely a greeting, leaving me to carry my own bag. The battered gladstone case banged against my knees as I climbed the servants' staircase to the third floor. Frank was right—it *was* heavy. But it contained all my essentials, including a dark worsted dress with a shortened train —ideal for quiet, after-hours movement—and my lockpicks. Frank had given me the picks as an anniversary gift five years before, when it became obvious that he could put my talents to good use. When we separated, I was tempted to dispose of that painful reminder of happier days. I don't know why I didn't. Perhaps I knew all along that I wasn't done with detecting.

The housekeeper threw open the door. I dropped my bag on the narrow bed in the corner and looked around the room.

"The maid's room will have to do for now," she said. "With the extra guests we're expecting for the cotillion, we're gonna be full up." She rested her hands on broad hips as she looked me up and down with a skeptical eye.

Frank had warned me about the housekeeper.

"The old battle-ax will probably be your biggest challenge," he'd said. "That woman watches everything and everybody. She wouldn't let me go anywhere beyond the parlor whenever I reported to Comstock. That's why I need you living and working at the mansion. You'll have a better chance to poke around than I ever could. Still, it isn't going to be easy."

I smiled brightly at the woman, hoping to work my way into her good graces. "This will be fine, Mrs. Koch, thank you."

She sniffed and regarded me over the rim of her spectacles. "Mr. Comstock is expecting you in the library as soon as you're settled. I hope you were minding where it was, 'cause we're all too busy getting ready for the horde that's gonna be descending on us tomorrow. I can't be coddling you and showing you around everywhere."

So much for Mrs. Koch's good graces. After assuring the woman that I could fend for myself, she muttered under her breath and closed the door behind her.

I changed quickly out of my traveling outfit and hid my lock-picks from prying eyes, behind the lowest drawer of the bureau. I headed for the main staircase. It might be the longer route to the library, but I hoped to familiarize myself with the house and avoid surprises while reconnoitering after-hours tonight. From what I had seen of the opulence of the foyer, with its stained-glass clerestory windows, brass urns, and marble everywhere—right down to a nude statue of Venus—it would not do to knock over a suit of armor or some other ridiculous symbol of affluence while groping along a dark hallway. It seemed the Comstocks had more money than they knew of ways to spend it.

I passed a number of closed bedroom doors. I'd been surprised when Frank told me that Leonard Frasier actually lived with the Comstocks. Apparently he'd moved in shortly after the death of his wife several years ago and had stayed ever since. No doubt it was convenient for H.A. Comstock, too, if a business matter came up after hours. I would certainly be searching Frasier's rooms when I had the chance.

A pretty little blonde-haired maid, arms full of linens, was just coming out of one of the bedrooms. I had an idea. "Excuse me?" The girl nearly dropped her stack. "Oh!" She looked up. "You startled me, miss. Are you the new assistant for the master?"

"Yes. I'm Miss Hamilton."

"I'm Elise," she said. "What can I do for you?"

I fished in my pocket for my stenographer's pad and held it up. "Mr. Comstock wanted me to leave this on Mr. Frasier's desk. Where are his rooms?"

I followed Elise's glance as she nodded toward the set of doors near the landing. "Over there. But I'm afraid you can't get in," she said. "Mr. Frasier keeps his rooms locked whenever he's out of town." She shifted the heavy stack of linens in her arms and held out a hand. "But I can put it on his desk for you."

I slipped the pad back into my pocket. "Never mind, but thank you. So Mr. Frasier is out of town?"

"He comes back tomorrow," Elise said. "If there's nothing else, would you excuse me? I have more beds to take care of."

"Of course."

As I approached the top of the staircase, I noticed a young man in his early twenties standing at the bottom, grinning up at me. He was well-formed and muscular, with broad shoulders and a strong jaw. There was a bandage on his left temple, along with several scrapes upon the left side of his face. It could only be Comstock's son, Gerard.

"So you are the lady who is to help my father," he called up to me. He shook his head in mock resignation. "He's still writing that musty old history of the *illustrious* Comstocks."

I said nothing as I continued down the stairs toward him. He didn't give ground as I approached the bottom step.

"I thought he'd hired a prune-faced old crone." He looked me up and down with a brazen leer. "You're a tall one—and I'd say that's a rather stubborn-looking chin—but you'll do. My week has improved immensely."

I returned his stare with an icy one of my own. "I'll overlook your impertinence," I retorted, "seeing as it was, indeed, a difficult week for you. Stand aside, if you please."

Gerard unconsciously put a hand to his bandage and scowled. "What the devil do *you* know about it?"

"That's enough," came a stern voice from across the hall. To the right of the staircase a door had opened, and there stood Henry Altree Comstock, glowering at his son. "Let Miss Hamilton alone."

Gerard gave me one last glare for good measure before barely moving aside. I kept my face expressionless as I brushed past him.

"Aren't you accompanying your sister to her riding lesson?" Comstock asked his son. "You'd best get changed."

With a sullen look, Gerard left, his heels ringing angrily on the marble floor.

A difficult young man, to say the least. Had recent events put a strain upon Gerard, or did a long-standing animosity exist between father and son? The young man's unsubtle eye for the ladies could be part of the trouble between them, although I sensed there was something more.

"This way," Comstock said, holding open the door.

The library was a welcoming place, with its richly paneled walls, deep oak bookcases, and gently worn leather chairs. A fire burned brightly in the grate, dispelling the chill and damp of the November afternoon.

"Be seated," he said, waving to a chair and closing the door firmly behind him. I could see the son's resemblance in the father, with his muscular build and wide shoulders. Both sported a well-defined jaw, although Comstock's had jowled with age.

"We have a mutual acquaintance named Frank Wynch who recommended I hire you, Miss Hamilton. *Hmm...Hamilton....*" He looked me over with a doubtful eye. "Surely you are not connected to the *Boston* Hamiltons?"

I knew this was coming. I let out a breath and shook my head.

"Not in the least. Our family is of a humbler background. Perhaps there is some distant connection of which I am unaware."

Comstock's frown cleared. "I suppose. Well then, let us proceed. Would you state clearly, please, what you understand your duties to be?"

"Regarding what is known to your family and associates, I am engaged to assist you in completing your history of the Comstock family. I will compile notes, take dictation, and so on." I pulled out my stenography notebook and set it on the side table. "I'm fully prepared to act in that capacity."

"And your other duties?" Comstock prompted.

"Known only to us three—you, Mr. Wynch, and myself—I'm here to find definitive proof of the person behind the factory sabotage and the death of the messenger boy. Mr. Wynch tells me you suspect Michael Broadhurst, your business rival." I hesitated, remembering Frank's warning, yet reluctant to keep secrets from my own employer. "Can you think of anyone else we should consider?"

Comstock's brow creased. "Wynch told you about Leonard Frasier's tie clasp, didn't he? It could have fallen off at any time. Or someone could have dropped it to implicate him." He shook his head. "Leonard has served Comstock Industries admirably over the years. I've known the man since our college days."

That hardly cleared Leonard Frasier from suspicion. Loyal friendships can sour more easily than wary associations between business competitors.

"Wouldn't Mr. Frasier profit from your death, sir?" I pointed out.

"Not a penny, and he would likely be out of a job," Comstock said tersely.

I gave him a startled glance. "'Out of a job'? Doesn't Frasier take over the company in the event of your death?"

"Where did you hear that? My will leaves everything to my son."

"There is no other will?" I asked, confused. How did Frank get that wrong?

Comstock sighed. "In a fit of pique, I did draft a will to leave the factory and shipping line to Leonard. There would have been enough left of our other investments for my family to live comfortably. That was *supposed* to be confidential, young lady." He frowned in disapproval.

"A draft? Nothing has been finalized?"

"Correct. I'll probably never sign that will."

"When was this? Did Mr. Frasier know about it?" I asked.

"A month ago. I told no one." Comstock's brow creased. "Obviously, a conversation with my attorney about client confidentiality is in order."

"May I ask why you drafted such a document cutting off your son?" I asked.

"I don't care to answer such an impertinent question, Miss Hamilton. It is a private matter."

At the sight of his clenched hands, I decided to soften my approach. "Every family, even affluent ones, has its difficult relations," I said quietly. "It seems to me that you have been carrying this burden alone for quite a while. Won't you tell me about it?"

Comstock looked at me for a long moment. I waited.

Finally, he gave a resigned sigh. "Several weeks ago, Gerard and I had a particularly bitter argument over his lack of involvement in the company." He got up and paced. "Our relationship has always been...difficult. He sneers at the family's legacy and my sense of responsibility toward the town of Rose Glen. He cares only for his own amusements. Should he inherit, he would sell the mill. I know it. Probably to Broadhurst, who would salvage the equipment and inventory and leave an empty shell. It would decimate the town's livelihood."

"And yet you won't sign the new will, but instead retain Gerard as your heir?" I asked.

"I want to keep it in the family. It is our legacy, after all. I'm hoping Gerard will have a change of heart."

I made no comment. The future of the mill was Comstock's problem. Finding the saboteur was mine. I still planned to search through Leonard Frasier's rooms tonight, but I was now convinced I needed to look further afield. Although Leonard may have learned of the new will, it seemed unlikely that he would act before it was finalized. Frank's theory, built on a tie clasp and an unsigned will, was rapidly falling apart.

"Tell me more about Michael Broadhurst," I said. "You believe he wants to drive you out of business in order to buy out your assets and eliminate you as competition, correct? Is he so ruthless that he's willing to kill you in order to do that?"

Comstock spread out his hands in a gesture of helplessness. "I would not have thought so before last week. He's a likable fellow. Our daughters are quite close, too. Both his daughter and mine are debutantes at this week's cotillion. The family visits often. He, his wife, and daughter were here just two weeks ago—the girls had dress fittings and plans to finalize. Everyone got along splendidly."

"And there was no unusual incident or threat to your life at that time?"

Comstock shook his head.

I considered this as I watched the play of firelight upon the hearth. Why the attempt on Comstock's life at the office, instead of in his home, a more convenient locale? Perhaps Broadhurst preferred hired hands to do his dirty work and keep himself clear of suspicion. However, such an approach made one vulnerable to blackmail.

"I understand that the Broadhursts arrive here tomorrow and stay the week?" I asked.

"Yes."

Why didn't Comstock rescind the invitation, if he believed Broadhurst was a physical threat to him? Social protocol in the face of such a risk was laughable. I raised a skeptical brow. "Is Broadhurst here merely for social purposes, or is there something more?"

Comstock smiled thinly. "How perceptive you are. Yes, he and I are in the midst of business negotiations."

"What sort of negotiations?"

"What does it matter? It can have no bearing upon the case."

"You cannot know that, sir. It's best if we have all available information. You needn't worry, Pinkerton operatives are bound by the strictest rules of confidentiality."

Comstock gave another sigh. "You are quite a persistent young lady. Very well. Broadhurst and I are considering a partnership to purchase a patent for making artificial silk."

"Artificial silk? I've never heard of such a thing."

"No one has made such a material successfully, though many have tried," he said. "Theo Vinet claims to have done so. I've seen preliminary reports that look quite promising. The man has been in the textile business for decades, first in France, then in New Orleans. The Southern mills have the benefit of plentiful raw materials and cheap labor, but lack the sophisticated equipment to produce the high-end fabrics we can make here. Vinet arrives tomorrow as well and will stay with us during the negotiations."

"So, even though you think Broadhurst is sabotaging your mill and trying to kill you, you are still planning to accept him into your home and proceed with this business venture?" I asked dryly.

Comstock's face grew dusky red. "Wynch has assured me that he can keep me safe outside of the house. Broadhurst would not dare try anything in my own home. Suspicion would point too quickly to him."

I suppressed a sigh. The man's arrogance was astonishing, but there was no help for it. "What do you want me to do?"

"As distasteful as it is to breach the trust between guest and host"—Comstock grimaced—"I want you to search through whatever papers Broadhurst brings with him. Your best opportunity will be when the entire household is at the cotillion the day after tomorrow. Even the staff will be given the evening off. You're looking for evidence of the saboteurs he hired and what else he may have planned. I suspect he set this in motion during his visit two weeks ago. The first incident at the factory was barely a week after that. He may use this visit to meet once again with his hirelings and pay them off. He must have cash for those he hired, and perhaps some record of who they are. When you find the proof, bring it to me."

"What will you do with the evidence?" I had a bad feeling about this.

Comstock's bitter smile made me shiver. "Use it to my advantage in my partnership with Broadhurst, of course. Perhaps a greater percentage of the profits from Vinet's invention? There are a number of possibilities."

"You're playing a dangerous game," I warned.

He gave me a look of barely disguised impatience. "It is my game to play, Miss Hamilton." He stood. "In the meantime, why don't I show you my memoir notes. I must concede they are in need of better organization."

Henry Altree Comstock may be a formidable industrial magnate, but his filing skills were sadly lacking. I had just approached him about yet another scrap of paper with no heading on it when there was a knock upon the library door.

"Simon! Come in," Comstock said, opening the door wider. He gestured to me. "Miss Hamilton, this is Simon Dwyer, my man at the mill. He can fix anything. We would be lost without him."

Simon Dwyer was a barrel-chested man in his sixties, with a heavily-creased face and thinning snow-white hair. His profound limp slowed him little as he crossed the room.

"I'm pleased to make your acquaintance, Mr. Dwyer," I said.

Dwyer took my hand briefly in his large, calloused one and gave an awkward bow over it. "As am I, miss." His voice had a soft Irish lilt.

"How are the repairs on the power loom coming?" Comstock asked.

Dwyer frowned. "Slow, sir. I repaired the gears. Smithy's making a new treadle. We still have to replace a number o' heddle wires. A tangled mess they are."

Comstock clasped him on the shoulder. "If anyone can fix it, you can."

Dwyer nodded. "If you can spare me now, Mrs. Koch tells me the stove in't drawing properly and your cook is in a dither."

"Yes, yes, by all means. My wife would die of mortification if dinner is undercooked," Comstock said with a wink.

Dwyer gave another little bow in my direction and left.

"He seems a nice man," I said.

Comstock smiled. "Salt of the earth. Comstock Industries would not be what it is today without him. He has been with us for more than four decades, except for the brief time he served in the war. My grandfather hired him as a lad. He really should retire, but how would I manage without him? As you can see, he not only attends to the factory, but takes care of things that break down in the house."

"How did he come by his limp?"

"Wounded on Stoneman's Raid, in the middle years of the war," Comstock said.

I nodded. "The Chancellorsville Campaign." Noting Comstock's astonished expression, I added, "My brother is an eager scholar of the subject."

Comstock sighed. "The war was a sad chapter in our country's history, Miss Hamilton. Simon's only son, Connor, was killed during that raid. He was a mere boy of seventeen, but keen to serve in the 1st Massachusetts Cavalry alongside his father."

"How horrible. It must have been devastating for Dwyer's wife."

Comstock shook his head. "She died giving birth to Connor. That boy was his whole life. But the entire town rallied around Simon when he came back at the end of '63, made sure he didn't want for anything. He is beloved by the townspeople and would do anything for them in return."

Comstock checked the mantel clock. "Can you manage on your own? I have other things to attend to before dinner."

"Of course."

CHAPTER 3

I met the remainder of the family, Mrs. Comstock and her daughter Sally, just before dinner. Mrs. Comstock seemed polite enough, as dictated by good breeding, but little more. She was petite, even for a woman. I felt positively gargantuan standing beside her. It would not do for a subordinate to sit in the presence of the lady of the house unless she was bidden to do so—and I was not—so I spent the before-dinner conversation gazing down upon the graying roots of the lady's tinted hair.

It had been a long time since I had last been among affluent society, and I'd forgotten how well known my family was among the New England blue-blood set. Mrs. Comstock soon tired of engaging me in discussion once I told her that I was in no way related to the Boston Hamiltons. Thank heaven the name *Hamilton* is not an unusual one.

Sally Comstock was a fresh-faced girl of fifteen, tall like her father, and radiated youthful energy. Although she had an unfashionable sprinkling of freckles across her cheeks, her glossy brown hair and fine figure would secure her no end of dance partners, I was sure.

Dinner was to be a quiet affair, no doubt in anticipation of greater revelry in the coming days. I was relieved to learn that Gerard had an engagement elsewhere. For the time being, I was to be spared the young man's leers and impertinent personal comments.

Cotillion talk resumed once we were seated at the dinner table.

"The event will be the highlight of the Season," Mrs. Comstock said, glancing in my direction, no doubt wondering if I knew what a cotillion was. I had, of course, attended more than my share of balls and other entertainments, but my days of privileged leisure were most certainly behind me, whether I was a boarding-house landlady, a personal assistant to a millionaire, or an aspiring lady Pinkerton. I affected wide-eyed awe at the matron's pronouncement.

Sally interjected eagerly. "Oh, Miss Hamilton, you should see the dress I'm to wear! It is white silk with a cross-bodice in the palest tint of ice peach, and a luxurious train…." Her voice trailed off at a sharp look from her mother. I smiled into my napkin. I remembered being chided for unbridled enthusiasm at her age. The girl's spirit was infectious. I hoped her mamma wouldn't squelch it entirely.

"What will *you* be wearing, Miss Hamilton?" Sally resumed, in a more composed voice.

"Silly dear!" Mrs. Comstock cut across, before I could answer. "She's not attending the dance. You are making your debut within *our* proper social set."

Sally glanced at me with pink-tinged cheeks.

I smiled at the girl. "But I would love to see your gown. Then I can picture how lovely you will be that evening."

Sally's flush deepened. "You are too kind." She turned to her mother. "May I show Miss Hamilton the dress tonight?"

Mrs. Comstock rolled her eyes and gave a mighty sigh. "I suppose."

After dinner, the gown was carefully unwrapped, inspected in great detail, and exclaimed upon.

Sally finally put it away. "I hope I don't embarrass my parents at the dance."

"Why would you think that?" I asked.

The girl shrugged. "I've been taking dancing lessons with Master Bernard for months, but I'm still awful. At yesterday's lesson, I stepped all over his feet as he scolded me in French."

I suppressed a smile. "I'm sure you'll do fine."

She flopped on the bed and looked over at me. "You're even taller than I am. May I ask you a personal question?"

"Of course."

"Do you find it terribly awkward to dance with gentlemen who are shorter than you? I imagine my partner staring at my bosom the entire time."

I chuckled. "I believe the discomfort is more the gentleman's. I leave him to sort out his own feelings."

The girl looked at me with anxious eyes. "You aren't too disappointed to miss the dance, are you?"

"Of course not." I smiled. "I have plenty of work to do, anyway."

"You're very nice. I hope we can be friends."

"Certainly we can," I said, realizing she must be rather lonely, a rich girl in a small mill town, surrounded by hired tutors but having no day-to-day peers of her own. No doubt she would feel better when the Broadhursts and their daughter arrived tomorrow.

I glanced at my lapel watch. Nearly time to meet Frank and report. "I have to go. Thank you for showing me your dress."

I changed from my silk taffeta into my high-necked black worsted gown and tiptoed quietly down the back stairs. A quick look down the hall revealed a tray-laden Mrs. Koch emerging from the study. I waited. When her footsteps faded, I slipped through the French doors to the side garden, creeping along the shadows of the house until I reached the arbor.

"You're late." Frank stepped from behind the lattice and tossed his cigarette in the shrubbery.

"Sorry. I didn't want Mrs. Koch to see me. She might think I was engaged in some lovers' tryst."

Frank slipped a hand around my waist and pulled me close. "Well, you can be," he breathed. I caught a whiff of bourbon. "You look beautiful in the moonlight, Pen. It's been a long time."

I wrenched myself out of his grasp. "Let us stick to the business side of things, if you please." I kept my voice level, even though I was seething. So he'd started drinking again. This did not bode well for the assignment.

He reluctantly sat on a stone bench while I sat across from him on the other, out of reach.

"I'll search Frasier's rooms tonight, while he's out of town," I said. "However, unless I find something damning, we should no longer consider him a prime suspect."

Frank's eyes narrowed. "Why not?"

"He has nothing to gain from the sabotage to the factory, or Comstock's death. The will in Frasier's favor was drafted but never finalized. Comstock says he wrote it in anger toward his son. He doesn't intend to leave anything to Leonard Frasier."

Frank looked at me, stunned. "I was...so sure."

"We must re-trench," I said firmly. I passed him an envelope. "Here is my report, based on what Comstock has told me. It's precious little, I grant you, but the guests arrive tomorrow. I hope to learn more then. In the meantime, can you find out about a man named Theo Vinet? All I know is that he's an inventor and cloth manufacturer from New Orleans. Comstock and Broadhurst are about to enter into a business deal with him. It's in my report. Also, look into Gerard Comstock's situation, particularly if he has any debts, or personal...entanglements."

"The son?" Frank's voice was tinged with skepticism.

"Yes, I know, he was hurt in the office explosion, but an accomplice might have bungled the timing, or what day the bomb was to be set."

"What're you looking for?" Frank asked.

"Gerard strikes me as the type with expensive hobbies. Perhaps he has problems that a tidy inheritance would resolve."

Frank glanced over my report and sighed. "Well, back to where we started, I s'ppose. Jus' like old times, heh?" His speech was starting to slur.

Too much like old times. I grimaced in the dark.

"Why don't you get some sleep?" I suggested, getting up to leave. "You look...tired." *And stay away from the bottle,* I added silently. There was no point in confronting him about it. Sad experience had shown me that.

He chuckled and tucked the envelope in his pocket. "Don't you remember, dear? We're the watchful eyes of the Pinkerton Agency. *We never sleep.*"

"The real work will come after the Broadhursts arrive tomorrow," I reminded him. "Comstock will need your protection then." I prayed he could stay in control of himself until we were finished with the case. Then, he could drink himself to blazes for all I cared. Without waiting for a response, I left.

Mrs. Koch was fortunately nowhere to be seen as I made my way back to my room. I pulled my set of lockpicks from their hiding place and waited for the house to settle down for the night. I tried not to think of Frank and his drinking problem. The truth was I *did* still care about what happened to him. But what was I to do?

I dozed a little, and when it was well after midnight, I secreted the pick-case in a deep skirt pocket and ventured out. I brought along a small lantern, shuttered to give off a modicum of light. I kept to the side of the corridor to avoid the well-used creaky boards along the middle, taking care not to brush against the doors. It would not do for a light sleeper to be aroused to my presence.

Finally, I reached Leonard Frasier's rooms.

Both the dim light and my lack of recent practice with the picks made the job go slowly, and I was crouched outside the door far longer than I'd planned. By the time I got the door open and slipped inside, my hands were shaking and my heart thudded in my chest.

I began to explore, shining my lantern along the surfaces of Leonard's bedroom. Atop the bureau was a tray of toiletries— unremarkable. Judging from his hairbrush, Leonard must have retained the full head of wavy brown hair I remembered. The night-table held a pair of reading spectacles, a water tumbler, and a photograph. I looked at the latter more closely. I didn't recognize the woman. Most likely his deceased wife. I moved to the drawers, opening each one, and then felt around under the bedskirts. Nothing out of the ordinary.

I moved quickly to the connecting study. I wasn't necessarily in a hurry—with Leonard gone until tomorrow, I had all night to search—but I was exhausted. The sooner I finished here, the better. I knew I needed sleep in order to have my wits about me when he returned tomorrow. How was I to persuade him to go along with my story? Knowledge of my connection to the wealthy Boston Hamiltons could compromise my cover.

The study was spartan by the usual Comstock family standards. Desk, chair, reading chair, side table, and bookcase were all that occupied the room.

I felt around the bookcase, looking for hidden levers and hollowed-out book caches, carefully sliding out the books that looked well-handled. Nothing unusual.

I turned my attention to the desk and employed my picks again, this time with greater ease. I went through the drawers one by one, skimming through each paper and carefully putting it back. There was nothing untoward: business correspondence, receipts, quarterly reports. I even pulled the drawers out completely and felt beneath and behind for secreted papers.

The only unusual item was a locked box of smooth teak. I pulled out my tiniest lockpick and had it open in an instant. Inside was a bundle of faded envelopes, bound in a blue ribbon. I slid one out. My breath caught as I recognized the familiar hand. *Oh, Lord.*

Leonard had saved my love letters, written during our courtship. I riffled through the pile. There were two dozen or so, all from me. No letters from any other woman, including his dead wife.

I don't know how long I stood there, gaping at my hand-writing on the envelopes, before the sound of footsteps roused me. I quickly restored the bundle, locked the box, put it back in the drawer, and locked the desk.

My breath caught when I heard the bedroom door open in the next room and saw a light under the connecting door.

It must be Leonard, I thought in a panic. How could he be back *now*, in the middle of the night?

The footsteps were coming closer. None of the sparse furnishings would hide me. I slipped into the corner beside the door hinges—which mercifully opened inward—and waited. The door opened nearly to my face, shielding me from the light spilling in from the other room. I couldn't see him from my vantage point, but I heard him move toward the desk, then a *thunk* of a briefcase being dropped upon it. The footsteps moved back into the bedroom.

He didn't close the door.

My chest constricted. How would I get out of here? With the door open, I didn't dare walk across the study to the hall door. I was trapped until he fell asleep.

I peered through the door hinge crevice, watching him moving around the bedroom. The years had been kind to him. He had indeed retained his thick hair of wavy brown, only slightly touched by silver. The compact, muscled frame hadn't yet paunched around the middle. His face, however, had not gone unscathed by the years. The shadowed eyes, the lined forehead— these spoke of fatigue, as well as past sorrow and strain.

I breathed an inaudible sigh as I watched him pull a nightshirt out of the armoire. He was retiring immediately. Thank heaven.

As a proper lady, I should have closed my eyes at that point. I did not. At least I had the decency to blush profusely as he dropped his trousers.

Finally Leonard turned down the lamp and climbed into bed. I waited until his breaths became slow and regular, then made my escape back to my own room.

I lay awake a long time, wondering how I was going to deal with Leonard Frasier.

CHAPTER 4

I overslept and got to the breakfast table late, incurring the reproachful frown of Mrs. Koch. The Comstocks had already eaten. There was no sign yet of Leonard. Good. That would give me a little more time to refine my story.

I apologetically passed Mrs. Koch the now-cold teapot. "Could I trouble you for more hot water?" With a dark mutter—something about *lady of leisure*—she left for the kitchen.

After breakfast I went to the library in search of Mr. Comstock. He wasn't there, but I decided to remain and continue organizing his notes. I had an idea for a cross-referenced index of symbols that would make the information easier to retrieve later. All the while, I listened for the sound of Leonard's voice. I hoped to intercept him and speak with him alone.

Nearly an hour had passed without interruption when I heard someone walk into the library. My chest constricted when I looked up to see Leonard Frasier, gaping at me with equal parts confusion and delight.

"Penelope?"

"Hello, Leonard," I said calmly, not feeling that way in the least.

"What on earth are *you* doing here?" he asked.

"There isn't much time," I answered, glancing anxiously toward the door. "I promise I will tell you the entire story later, but I need you to go along with me for a while."

He frowned.

"To the household, I am a lady of limited means, in need of gainful employment. I have specifically told the Comstocks that I am *not* related to the Hamiltons of Boston. I don't want to bring my family into this. My parents have suffered some...financial embarrassments recently. It's important that no one know."

Leonard regarded me in silence. I waited, holding my breath. The fabrication I'd considered so clever in the early morning hours now seemed a ridiculously transparent tissue of lies.

"You simply left without a word," he finally said, softly. "It took me a long time to get over that." His eyes narrowed. "So you are still 'Miss Hamilton.' You never married?"

My face reddened, remembering the love letters he kept carefully tucked away. I shook my head. "No." I hated that lie most of all.

There were footsteps in the hall. "Please, would you help me now?" I urged. "I promise to tell you all of it later."

Leonard hesitated as if to say something, then Comstock walked in.

"Ah!" Comstock said brightly, "I see you two have met." He turned to Frasier. "Miss Hamilton has already proved herself indispensable to my project." Leonard nodded politely but said nothing.

My knees quavered in my relief.

Comstock turned to me. "How are you getting on?"

I held up a notecard with a column of symbols. "Fine, sir. In fact, I'm implementing an easier system for your notes, which should—"

"Splendid, splendid," Comstock cut in, already turning aside. "Leonard, let us go to the study to talk. I'm eager to hear about your trip. Anything we can use in our negotiations with Vinet?"

Leonard gave one last doubtful look over his shoulder at me. "I think so," he answered, following Comstock through the door. "We'll have the unique advantage of...." His voice faded as they left the room. With a sigh, I went back to my notecards, not at all confident that Leonard would continue the charade for very long.

Mid-afternoon brought the chaos of guests arriving—heavy footsteps on the stairs, the banging of trunks, the babble of voices mixed with girlish squeals. I stayed where I was, reluctant to get swept up in the hubbub. Time enough to meet the newcomers at dinner.

In the meantime, I pulled out Frank's report in order to reacquaint myself with what I knew about Michael Broadhurst. Before focusing upon Leonard Frasier as the suspect, Frank had compiled a thorough history of Comstock's chief rival.

Although Michael Broadhurst was close in age to Comstock—both men in their mid-fifties—the backgrounds of the two were utterly different. Comstock was born of a long-standing philanthropic family, while Broadhurst had arisen out of a hardscrabble life in a New York tenement. His meteoric rise in the textile industry was the stuff of legend. Twenty years ago, Broadhurst had somehow acquired a run-down Pennsylvania textile mill and a goodly supply of cotton and other raw materials. How this came to be was unclear. Frank listed the rumors as including a high-stakes poker game, a well-placed bit of blackmail, and an inheritance from a distant relative. For a self-educated man such as Broadhurst, what he did with the company since then was astonishing. Strategic borrowing enabled him to renovate and buy the latest equipment. Back-room business alliances got him cut-rate deals on shipping. Wining and dining secured him the legal and business minds he needed to supplement his own lack of education. The old wreck of a mill was transformed into the thriving business that now rivaled Comstock Industries.

Wealth, the great social equalizer, had elevated the Broadhursts beyond Michael's humble beginnings, and despite the business rivalry between the men, the Comstock and Broadhurst families spent a great deal of time together. The proposed partnership to acquire Theo Vinet's patent for artificial silk would bind them further.

I folded the report and tucked it away. Broadhurst was our most promising candidate for the sabotage of Comstock's mill and the attempt on his life. The man's rough-and-tumble background, the sketchy circumstances under which he'd acquired the Pennsylvania mill...these pointed to someone who wasn't squeamish about employing unsavory means to get what he wanted.

"Miss Hamilton?" a tentative voice asked. It was Sally, accompanied by a petite, redheaded young lady.

I smiled. "Come in, please."

"Are we disturbing you?"

"Not at all."

"This is my friend, Enid," Sally said. Enid gave a shy smile and looked at me curiously. Perhaps she'd never seen a lady who worked for her living before. "We hoped you would join us in the parlor for tea."

"Mercy, is it that late?" I checked my watch. "I could do with a cup of tea, but are you sure your mother won't mind me joining your parlor guests?"

The girls nodded. "In fact," Enid Broadhurst piped up, "my mother was hoping you could keep Madame Vinet in conversation. Do you know French? It seems she doesn't speak much else, and Mamma's French has been quite exhausted by now."

I didn't realize Theo Vinet would be bringing a wife. "Of course." I stood and smoothed my navy wool skirt. It was purely a reflex. I was sure to look quite dowdy beside the society matrons. Little more was expected of a personal assistant.

We passed the corridor leading to the kitchen, where the sounds of clanging metal and masculine grumbling were unmistakable.

I stopped. "What on earth?"

Enid giggled behind her hand while Sally sighed. "The stove is acting up again. Simon's trying to fix it before supper. We won't have scones with our tea, but cook has made some lovely sandwiches."

"Perhaps you can play the pianoforte," I suggested with a wink, "to cover the noise." This time, both girls giggled.

Mrs. Broadhurst, a robust middle-aged woman with raven-black hair piled into absurd ringlets, gave me barely a glance as I walked in. She resumed the conversation with her hostess. "...and would you believe it? Sadie White has been positively *throwing* herself at her daughter's music instructor! I heard it from Mrs. Anderson...."

Madame Vinet looked up in curiosity as we approached. Sally gave a pretty little curtsy and made the introduction in her best schoolroom French.

Where Mrs. Broadhurst was plump and curved, Madame Vinet was all points and angles. Her face was dominated by a beaky nose, high bony cheeks, and a protruding jaw. The saving grace was her expressive dark brown eyes, large, luminous, and heavily outlined.

"*Bonjour, Madame,*" I said politely.

Madame Vinet's eyes lit up, and she gestured to the cushion beside her. "*Oh, mademoiselle, vous parlez francaise? Magnifique! Ces autre dames*"—she dropped her voice and looked over at the women—"*sont fatigues.*"

I looked over at the ladies in question, now enthusiastically conversing about tomorrow's dance. They didn't look at all "tired" of conversation. Madame Vinet was a born diplomat. I accepted a cup of tea from the maid as I perched beside Madame on the settee.

For the next half hour, against the backdrop of cotillion conversation and the sounds of stove-banging in the kitchen, Madame Vinet and I spoke of the weather, fashion, men—I had little to contribute to that part of the conversation—and her husband's invention.

"Ah," I said, "*l'invention* of your husband—*de votre mari*—is highly sought after—*tres recherche*."

"*Oui*." Madame spoke with bright, animated hand motions, explaining her husband's long hours away from home doing research, taking extended trips, pleading for funds. Her French was rapid. As fluent as I was, it was a challenge to keep up with her.

I was about to surreptitiously check the mantel clock when I noticed the ladies getting up from their seats. Time to dress for dinner. Mrs. Comstock gave me a meaningful look, and I dutifully translated for Madame Vinet.

"*Merci, Mademoiselle Hamilton*," Madame Vinet said, rising. "*J'ai apprécié notre petite conversation*."

I nodded. I'd enjoyed our chat, too.

Preparing for dinner was a simple affair for me, as it only involved changing my dress and smoothing my hair. I was the first one out of my room. I decided to take a stroll along the wing of guest bedrooms, to learn who occupied which rooms. It would save time later.

Through the closed doors just next to Leonard Frasier's rooms, I heard the chatter of French. The Vinets. Easy enough. I continued past the linen closet to the next set of doors. Just as I leaned in to listen, I heard a hand grasping the inner knob. Quickly, I took a few steps back, wrenched a hairpin from my head, and dropped it on the carpet.

Out came Mrs. Broadhurst, who started at the sight of me. "Oh!" Her eyes narrowed. "Whatever are you doing outside my daughter's door?"

I was bent over, looking along the floor. "Ah, *there* it is." I picked up the pin and straightened. "I do beg your pardon. I lost a pin." I smoothed back the loose strand and tucked the pin into place.

Mrs. Broadhurst gave a perfunctory nod, crossing the hall to the set of doors at the end.

Perfect. I smiled to myself as I headed downstairs.

No guests had yet come down. Perhaps I could peruse Comstock's extensive book collection in the meanwhile.

I hesitated at the closed library door. Should I knock? Then I heard a voice raised in anger—Comstock. I put my ear to the door, but the other man's voice was an unintelligible murmur. Vinet and his wife were upstairs. It didn't sound like Frank or Leonard. That left Broadhurst as the only possibility.

The sound of brisk footsteps—likely Mrs. Koch—forced me to abandon my post and hurry to the parlor to wait for the ladies. I didn't trust the hairpin trick to work a second time, especially with the housekeeper.

CHAPTER 5

*C*omstock ate little at dinner, though no one else seemed
to notice. Mrs. Comstock, Mrs. Broadhurst, and their
daughters talked excitedly about tonight's entertainment—a
concert, to be given at the same banquet hall as the cotillion
tomorrow evening. Comstock's son Gerard, whom I had not seen
since yesterday, was paying particular attention to Enid. He
looked positively amiable and was refreshingly well-behaved.

Vinet, Broadhurst, and Leonard were at the far end of the
table, discussing the business potential of artificial silk. I glanced
at Michael Broadhurst in curiosity. Based upon what I read of his
background, I admit I had expected a shady-looking man of
coarse mannerisms, likely to commit no end of *faux pas* among
this gently-born group. On the contrary, the short, pudgy man,
though over-fond of the sound of his own voice, was well spoken,
witty, and completely at his ease. It was difficult to conceive of
him as our primary suspect in the mill incidents. No doubt any
number of potential associates found it easy to trust such an
agreeable fellow—at their own risk, if the rumors about him were
to be believed.

Madame Vinet had been strategically placed across the table

from me. We talked of Parisian food and our favorite sights of that city.

"Do you miss—*manquez vous—Paris?*" I inquired, noting her thoughtful look.

She shook her head. "*Pas tant*—not much. Do you, *mademoiselle?*" she asked, with a mischievous gleam in her eye.

I realized, too late, that the hard-working Miss Hamilton should most certainly *not* be a frequent visitor to Paris, as I had been. I shrugged. "*Parfois.*" Sometimes.

Madame Vinet's expression turned sympathetic. "*Vous avez subi un changement de fortune, oui?*"

I nodded. Yes, I had suffered a change in fortunes, though not quite as she supposed.

"*Pourquoi travailler pour ces gens?*" she asked, her eyes narrowing. Why work for these people?

I couldn't tell her that. I merely shook my head.

Madame hesitated. "*Monsieur Comstock n'est pas un homme gentil.*" Not a nice man.

I lowered my voice. "It's more that...he's careful. *Il se garde.*"

Madame looked at me with narrowed eyes. "*Il a un secret.*" He has a secret.

I took a quick glance around the table before turning back to Madame Vinet. "A secret? What secret?" I whispered.

Madame ignored my question. "Come back...with me," she said in a low voice. "*Comme mon compagnon.*"

"As your companion?" I repeated, surprised. I shook my head. "*Merci, mais j'ai des devoirs ici.*" I have duties here.

I heard the scraping of chairs being pushed back. "Shall we proceed to the foyer?" Mrs. Comstock said in a strident voice. "It seems we have lingered a bit long over dinner. The carriages have arrived already."

Vinet, a wiry, dapper man in a bright paisley waistcoat, came over to help his wife out of her seat. Madame Vinet gave me a small smile as they headed for the foyer, leaving me with more questions than answers.

Leonard came around to my chair. "You're not going to the concert?" I asked, getting up. We made our way to the front staircase.

"Regretfully, no," he said. "I have a great many documents to read tonight in preparation for our negotiations with Vinet in the morning. I hope you weren't planning to occupy the library. I need room to spread out."

"Not at all," I said. "I intend to retire early. It has been a tiring day." I craned my neck to peer through one of the front windows of the foyer, hoping for a glimpse of Frank. As Comstock's security man, he would be driving the lead carriage for the concertgoers. I prayed he was alert tonight. Heaven help us if my husband had dipped into the bottle again.

My back stiffened as Leonard stepped close and touched my elbow. "Pen."

The statue of Venus blocked us from sight of the guests as they collected their wraps and hats. I looked over my shoulder at him.

He turned me toward him, hands lingering on my shoulders. "What's happened to you?" His gray eyes clouded with disapproval.

"I told you," I began, my heart hammering in my chest, "my family circumstances changed, and I—"

"No." He cut across my rehearsed speech. "That's not what I mean, although I have my doubts about your story. I do hear news of your family from time to time, and nothing about a misfortune has reached my ears. I mean, what has happened to *you*. You've changed. Distant. Impersonal. Self-contained. I used to be able to read your feelings, but now...." His voice trailed off.

I shrugged out of his grasp. This was just what I feared would happen. The man knew me too well, even after all these years.

He dropped his hands. "I used to be able to tell by your eyes, mostly. And there was an exuberance about you that was irresistible." His lips quirked as if he was smiling at a memory. But the memory faded, and his expression turned angry. "But you've grown a shell. Who did this to you?"

My eyes stung with unshed tears. "I've grown up," I croaked, pushing past him.

The tears came once I was safely back in my room. Thankfully, the storm quickly passed. I blew my nose and felt calmer.

Impersonal. Self-contained. If he only knew. But there was no point in dwelling upon it. I had a job to do. I changed into my dark dress once again and put the lockpicks in my pocket.

I quietly closed the door behind me and descended the servants' staircase for the second floor. Comstock had suggested I search Broadhurst's room when everyone was at the cotillion tomorrow night. However, if Broadhurst was planning to pay off an accomplice, the money might be gone by then and possibly other proof along with it. The servants were occupied in the kitchen. Leonard was safely out of the way in the library with his papers. I had perhaps an hour before Elise turned down the beds. That should be sufficient.

The guest room doors had locks that could only be secured from the inside, so I slipped into the Broadhursts' rooms without even having to reach for my picks. I spied the briefcase jutting out from under a pile of cast-off clothing—the Broadhursts were a rather slovenly couple, it seemed—but I left that until last. I first went around the suite of rooms, checking in drawers, behind furniture, and even the pockets of Broadhurst's discarded clothing, taking care to drop the items back where they had been.

Finally I turned to the briefcase. It was beautifully constructed of expensive black calfskin, but the locks were of shoddy quality. I soon had them open.

I sifted through inventory reports, shipping schedules, and monthly earnings statements. Nothing unusual. Near the bottom, however, I found two items of interest. The first was a wad of bills, neatly bound and encased in a cloth bag. I did a quick count:

five hundred dollars. Quite a sum. I replaced it and turned to the other item. It was an unsigned partnership agreement between Broadhurst and Comstock for the acquisition of Theo Vinet's artificial silk patent. The only thing remarkable about it was the proposed split of the profits: seventy percent to Broadhurst and only thirty percent to Comstock.

I frowned. Broadhurst was no fool—why would he have such a document drafted? He must know that Comstock would never agree to such an allotment. Unless...

Il a un secret, Madame Vinet had said.

I started at the sound of footsteps in the corridor outside. Elise must be starting early. Quickly, I restored the contents of the briefcase, secured the locks, and tucked the case back under the pile of clothes. I stood by the door, waiting. When a sufficient interval had elapsed with no sound, I opened the door.

Leonard Frasier waited outside.

"It appears you have some explaining to do," he said, arms crossed in front of his chest.

CHAPTER 6

$\mathcal{T}$he library had a cheery fire going, but I barely felt its warmth as I stood in front of it, trembling. How could I account for my presence in Broadhurst's room without telling him of my true position in the household? And I certainly wanted to leave out mention of Frank, for personal as well as professional reasons. Somehow, Leonard finding out that I was married to Frank Wynch bothered me a great deal.

Leonard poured two glasses of cognac and passed one to me. "Sit. Drink this. You look as if you need it."

To stall for time more than anything else, I complied. The warmth of the liquor going down my throat stopped my trembling.

"Now," he said, sitting down across from me, "what were you doing in Broadhurst's room? Petty larceny hardly seems your style."

I set aside my glass. "I wasn't there to steal anything. Surely you must know that."

"Then what in the Sam Hill *were* you doing there?"

I shook my head. "It's confidential. I cannot say." I met his eyes. "I'm asking you to trust me and keep this between us."

Leonard sat back in his chair, legs crossed, as if he were settling in for a long chat. His eyes had taken on a faraway look that I recognized as intense concentration. I perched on the edge of my chair and waited anxiously.

"You are asking quite a lot," he said finally.

"I know. Will you?"

Leonard drew in a breath to answer, but the sound of carriage wheels on the drive made us both pause. We heard the front doors opening and women's voices in the foyer.

And then a shot.

I bolted out of the room. The shot was followed by female shrieks. As I reached the foyer with Leonard close behind, Comstock and his son came in with my barely-conscious husband propped up between them. My stomach lurched at the red stain spreading beneath Frank's jacket. "What happened?"

"A sniper," Comstock said brusquely. "We never saw him."

Michael Broadhurst came in, his plump face flushed with exertion. "There's no sign of the shooter, but I heard a horse galloping away." He pointed through a window, toward a ridgeline beyond the gravel driveway. "From that direction."

Comstock motioned toward the door. "Tell the other driver to fetch Doctor Fanshawe, would you? He knows where to find him." Broadhurst ran back outside as quickly as his short legs could carry him.

"How bad is it?" I asked Frank.

He gave a weak smile. "It's just the shoulder. I'll be fine."

I pretended to look, taking the opportunity to whisper to him without drawing anyone's attention. "Since you're in good hands, I'm going out to look around. I'll be back to report." Frank nodded.

I hung back from the chattering group of ladies milling about, then slipped out of the house, hoping no one would notice my absence.

I still wore my dark dress and sturdy-heeled shoes, which

made it easier to keep to the shadows and reconnoiter the uneven ground. If Michael Broadhurst was to be believed, the shooter was long gone, but it was best to be cautious. As I searched, I wondered. Why Frank? If the assassin had hit Frank by mistake, why not fire a second shot to kill Comstock?

Once I found the place, I could see it was ideal for the shooter's purpose. It had the proper elevation and was situated about a hundred yards from the house. Sufficient vegetation screened one from view of the road but did not obstruct the line of sight. The dirt trail just beyond would make it easy to slip away without encountering the main road. I saw recent evidence of the horse Broadhurst had heard, although no shoe indentations were to be seen on the frozen ground.

I checked the area as thoroughly as I could in the scant light. Several cigarette stubs littered the ground beside a boulder. The shooter had sat there, waiting a long time for his target. I placed one in my handkerchief, although I didn't hold out high hopes for it being anything but a common brand. Hunting further, I found the spent brass rifle casing, which I also put in my handkerchief. I slipped the bundle into my pocket.

"There you are," a voice said. Leonard Frasier stepped out of the shadows.

"What are you doing here?" I asked, my voice sounding shaky to my own ears. The man had an annoying habit of coming upon me unawares.

"When I noticed you missing from the hallway, I had a hunch you were out here." He frowned. "Rather reckless of you, Pen."

I shrugged. "It seemed doubtful the shooter would linger. I wanted a look at the scene." I shivered and hugged my arms. "Although I wish I'd stopped for a shawl."

Leonard took off his jacket and put it over my shoulders. I breathed in the spicy scent of his sandalwood aftershave. "Thank you," I said, blushing.

He took a step back and surveyed me with a critical eye. "Why am I finding you in the most unlikely places for a lady to be? You are no mere 'assistant,' are you? I want the whole story. No more evasions. Why were you in Broadhurst's room? Why are you the first person to come here to look around?"

I kicked aside a pebble, keeping my eyes on the ground. "I don't know what you're talking about."

He ground his teeth in exasperation. "If that's how you want to play it, I'll have to go to Comstock and recommend you be dismissed." He turned to leave.

"He knows all about me," I called after him. *Well, almost everything.*

Leonard stopped and turned back with a frown. "Go on."

I looked into his steady gray eyes. Could I trust him? I was maneuvering by intuition now. The Pinkerton detective manual contained nothing about dealing with an old flame. If Leonard carried out his threat and talked to Comstock about me, he would find out about my assignment anyway. At least I could save myself the embarrassment of Comstock learning that I had allowed myself to get caught. Perhaps, too, I could learn more from Leonard by taking him into my confidence. I took a breath to steady myself and began my tale.

To give him credit, he listened quietly, without interruption. I told him of my current assignment working with Frank Wynch, the theory of Broadhurst's involvement, and Comstock's request that I search Broadhurst's belongings to find evidence of his connection to the sabotage incidents. I left out the fact that Leonard had been Frank's primary suspect and that I had been in the room when he'd returned last night. I blushed at the memory.

Leonard frowned when I had finished. "How did you come to be investigating a case alongside a Pinkerton detective? It's a sordid business for a woman."

I didn't respond, doubting he would understand the fascination I felt for detective work. And I certainly was not going to unburden myself to him about my precarious finances.

During my silence, Leonard's expression softened. He gathered my hands in his. "I want to keep you safe, Pen. I still care for you, you know."

Oh, this was trouble. I realized I would have to tell him *all* of it. "I'm married to Frank Wynch," I said abruptly.

He dropped my hands and took a step back.

"We are living apart. There were...problems...that were irreconcilable." Why was I telling him this? None of that mattered. I was married. That was all.

Leonard's forehead creased in concern. "I'm sorry for your trouble, Pen, I truly am. You should be freeing yourself of Wynch for good, not getting involved in his assignment. Why did you take this on? Were you hoping to...reconcile with your husband?"

I gave an unbecoming snort. "No. I have no illusions about Frank. It's simply that we've worked together in the past, and he needs my help now. Speaking of which, could you do me a favor?"

Leonard gave me a look of mock exasperation. "*Another* favor?"

I smiled. "No one else knows that Frank and I are married. Not even Comstock. We've found it gives us greater flexibility to work a case that way. I would be grateful if you kept it to yourself."

He hesitated. "Very well. I see no harm in it."

I breathed a sigh and checked my watch. "We should be getting back."

Leonard took a final look around. "So, this is the spot. Whoever it was chose well. Did you find anything?"

"Cigarette butts and the rifle shell. I'll show Frank when we return to the house." I pointed to a tree a few feet away. "That's where the shooter tethered his horse. See the droppings and trampled weeds?"

He nodded, then followed me as I started back to the house. "What will you do now?" he asked.

"I'll search again in the morning. Perhaps I'll find something else in better light."

"Good idea. I'll accompany you," Leonard said.

I stiffened. "That isn't necessary. I'm perfectly capable of doing it myself."

"Your resourcefulness is already abundantly clear," Leonard said with a smile. "Consider me merely a gentleman whose services are at your disposal."

I relaxed, giving him a grateful glance. It was reassuring to have another ally. Detecting can be a lonely business.

∾

I found Frank with Comstock in the study. The doctor was just tidying up after bandaging Frank's shoulder and putting a sling on his arm. I was gratified to see that some color had returned to Frank's face. Only the deep shadows under his eyes gave away his pain and exhaustion.

"Rumor has it that you will live, Mr. Wynch," I said lightly. Frank gave me a wan smile, then frowned at the sight of Leonard's jacket still around my shoulders. I flushed and took it off.

The doctor turned to Frank on his way out. "Remember, no strenuous activity for the next few days." Frank gave a reluctant nod as the doctor left.

I looked from Frank to Comstock. "Tell me how it happened."

Comstock leaned back wearily in his chair. "The carriage with the Broadhursts and Vinets arrived here ahead of ours. The men waited outside as our carriage pulled up and helped my wife and daughter out of the vehicle. Gerard and I got out as well, and I'd just turned to give parting instructions to Wynch here, when we heard the shot and saw him crumple. Fortunately, the ladies were inside by then."

"So you, your son, and Mr. Wynch were standing together in a group?" I asked.

Comstock nodded.

I turned to Frank. "Is that how you remember it?"

"Yes."

Obviously the shooter had a clear shot of all three men. Was Frank the intended victim, then, with the goal being to maim rather than kill? I had the feeling we were dealing with a skilled sniper.

"Did you find anything?" Frank added, breaking into my thoughts.

"It's precious little." I pulled out my handkerchief and showed him what I'd collected. I described the location and the presence of the horse.

Frank picked up the shell and examined it closely.

"Can you tell what kind of rifle it came from?" I asked.

"Looks like a .52 caliber," Frank said. "Could be an old Spencer repeating rifle, although a Spencer carbine is more likely, if he got away on a horse. Rifles are too cumbersome to carry on horseback." He set down the casing with a sigh. "Doesn't narrow it down much. A lot of those around since the war. It's a good weapon."

"Accurate at a hundred yards?" I asked.

"And more," Frank said.

"Then how did you come to be hit instead of Mr. Comstock?" I asked.

"The moon was clouded over tonight," Frank pointed out. "He may not have had a clear view. The three of us were standing close together, and we're all of similar height."

Comstock, who had been silent all the while, stood. "I want to end this investigation, now."

"What!" I exclaimed. "Why? You need *more* protection, not less. It could have been you, or one of your children, or your wife, who had been struck by a bullet tonight. Why do you want to pull out of this now?"

Comstock shook his head stubbornly. "I want to take...a different approach. One that will not involve the Pinkerton Agency," he added, looking over at Frank.

I frowned, trying to make sense of this. Comstock must know

who was responsible. Perhaps his "different approach" involved an assassination of his own? This was not the Wild West. No Pinkerton would stand for such a course of action. I glanced over at Frank, who met my eye. No doubt he was thinking the same thing. We had to stall for time and find definitive proof of the guilty party before Comstock took matters into his own hands. And, of course, keep Comstock safe from the assassin's bullet in the meanwhile. I gave Frank a pointed look, waiting for him to take the lead.

Frank cleared his throat. "Give us one more day, sir."

Comstock looked over in surprise. "You haven't caught him after all this time, and now you're wounded. What difference will a day make?"

"The cotillion is tomorrow," Frank said. "I'll be bringing in more men to keep you and your family safe. My injury won't stop me from being there, despite what that doc wants. Doctors mollycoddle over every little scratch."

"I don't want to be surrounded by armed guards at my daughter's debut! What will my guests think?" Comstock said, raising his voice in agitation.

"No, no, it would be nothing like that," Frank said. "This man has tried two methods: explosives and a rifle. We will scour the building and grounds in advance for any hidden devices and merely monitor the entrances during the dance so that no one can slip in with a weapon. We can dress the men in wait-staff livery so they won't look conspicuous."

"In the meantime," I interposed, "I'll search for concrete evidence of Broadhurst's guilt." Was it my imagination, or did Comstock blanch at my mention of the name? "I had the chance to look through his briefcase while everyone was at the concert tonight." I described the money and partnership agreement I'd found. Frank looked intrigued, but Comstock didn't seem as pleased as I would have expected.

"Do you know why Broadhurst would bring such a document?" I asked Comstock.

Comstock rose. "We'll discuss this tomorrow. It's been a long night. If you will excuse me."

Frank and I watched him leave. "He's hiding something," Frank said finally.

I couldn't agree more. "Did you learn anything about Gerard Comstock and Theo Vinet?"

Frank shook his head. "Nothing yet on Vinet. I'm still waiting on my source in New Orleans. But your hunch was right about Gerard. He's racked up a number of gambling debts."

Interesting. Perhaps Gerard was more clever than I gave him credit for. The Comstock inheritance was sufficient motivation for a cash-strapped young man to be devious. But was he a cold-blooded killer, willing to allow a messenger boy to be killed in the process?

"I also heard something about a mistress in Boston," Frank continued, "but there's been no time to confirm if that's true." He scowled. "We'll be dismissed by Comstock before I can find out. We need *more time*."

"Time is a luxury we do not have at the moment," I said. "Where are you staying tonight? You shouldn't travel in your condition."

"Frasier offered his study. Mrs. Koch is setting up a cot for me."

I got up to leave, and Frank grasped my hand.

"I want you to know...I didn't have a drop tonight." Frank's voice was thin with pain. "I was alert. I was doing my job." He gave a bitter laugh. "Not that it did any good."

I patted his hand in reassurance. "I understand."

He hung onto my hand. "Pen, I'm sorry about last night. Truly. Before then, I hadn't had any liquor since the day you threw me out. I swear."

I hesitated, skeptical. "So why last night?"

He pulled me closer, tracing his thumb along the fine bones of my wrist, as he used to do. I suppressed a shiver. "Seeing you yesterday," he said, "after three years apart. You were right there, and yet unreachable. I couldn't bear it."

I waited silently.

"But I'm back in control now," he continued. He looked intently at my face, searching for my response, his eyes warm with emotion. "I promise it will never happen again. Pen, I love you. Take me back."

I promise it will never happen again. Take me back. Three years was not enough time to erase the memory of those oft-repeated words. Those broken promises.

Not trusting myself to speak, I pulled my hand away and left the room.

CHAPTER 7

I slept badly that night and woke late again, hurriedly dressing and heading downstairs to the breakfast room. No doubt Mrs. Koch would be convinced that I possessed delusions of grand living.

This time I wasn't the only one late to breakfast. Enid and Sally were helping themselves to the toast rack.

"Miss Hamilton, wasn't it an exciting evening?" Sally commented.

I smiled. "I did not attend the concert, so I cannot say."

"No, not the concert—that was an absolute bore," Sally said. "I mean the shot we heard. Everyone was in an uproar. But we didn't get to see what happened. Mrs. Koch hustled us away too quickly."

"Do *you* know what happened?" Enid asked.

"What did your parents tell you?" I countered warily. Although the girls looked to be of sturdy constitution, heaven forbid I send the young ladies into an attack of the vapors.

"Papa told me the groundskeeper had to kill a rabid raccoon," Sally said, with a skeptical look at her friend.

"Then that must be what happened," I said briskly.

She sighed, no doubt recognizing adult collusion when she saw it.

I changed the subject. "I imagine you two are looking forward to the dance tonight."

"I'm a bit nervous," Enid admitted.

"Me, too," Sally said. "But excited—so many people are coming! Papa has a special train, just for the guests traveling from New York."

Impressive, though hardly surprising.

"Miss Hamilton, would you come to Sally's room tonight and help us get ready?" Enid asked.

I smiled. "I wouldn't miss it."

I left the young ladies to their discussion of what jewels and ribbons they were to wear and went in search of Leonard to accompany me to the clearing. I shouldn't wait much longer to examine the area, in case someone came along and disturbed any evidence I'd missed. I found myself looking forward to spending time with him.

Leonard wasn't in the library, Comstock's study, or the parlor. Finally, I knocked on the door to his rooms.

"He's gone, miss," a soft voice said. I turned and saw Elise approach with a basket of mending under her arm.

I swallowed my disappointment. "Do you know where?"

"No, miss. It were peculiar, though, 'cause he left in an awful hurry and looked worried."

"When was this?" I asked.

Elise puckered her lips in thought. "'Bout two hours ago, I'd say."

Bother. Just before I'd come down to breakfast. "Did he say when he would return?" Surely he would be back for today's patent negotiations.

The girl shook her head.

"What about Mr. Wynch? Is he still here? I understand he stayed the night in Mr. Frasier's study."

"That he did," Elise said with a nod, "but Mr. Frasier tol' me the man was already gone 'afore he woke up."

Frank must be feeling better. I knew he had much to do in order to prepare for tonight, though I wished he hadn't left so soon. He still didn't know about Leonard Frasier and me. Last night had certainly not been the right time for *that* conversation.

Surely Comstock would know where Leonard was. I caught him just as he was about to join Broadhurst and Vinet in the library.

"Excuse me, sir, but isn't Mr. Frasier supposed to be in this meeting?" I asked.

Comstock frowned in annoyance. "Not that it's any concern of yours, but Mr. Frasier had an urgent personal matter that required his attention. If you'll excuse me, I cannot keep the others waiting."

Still troubled, I grabbed my fur-lined basque and headed to the clearing. Why did Leonard leave so abruptly, just before crucial negotiations with Vinet? Why did he leave without a note to me about his change in plans?

When I reached the clearing, a disquieting thought stopped me in my tracks. Could Leonard Frasier be involved after all? We had been together when the shot rang out, but he could have hired an accomplice. Perhaps Leonard feared I was getting too close to the truth. Had he left in haste this morning so as to warn off the shooter?

I did not want to believe it of Leonard. Why would he want Comstock dead? He had nothing to gain monetarily. In fact, he would be out of a job once Gerard inherited and sold the mill to Broadhurst, who by all accounts would promptly dismantle it.

Perhaps there was a personal reason, and Leonard was just playacting the role of Comstock's devoted friend and right-hand man. I had to admit that it would explain Comstock's decision to abruptly end the investigation. If he realized that Leonard Frasier, his best friend, was behind the factory sabotage and the attempts to kill him, he would want to handle it privately. But handle it how?

It also weighed heavily upon me that I had not been honest with Frank. Not only had I withheld the fact that Leonard Frasier and I had a history, I also hadn't told him that Leonard now knew all about our investigation. I sighed. I would never forgive myself if I'd tipped our hand to the would-be murderer.

My best course was to ask Comstock point-blank about his relationship with Leonard. I hadn't noticed a strain between them, but who could say for sure? I also resolved to send a message to Frank if Leonard did not return. No doubt Frank would be furious with me once he knew the whole story.

I made no progress that day—the last day Frank and I were given to solve the case before Comstock dismissed us. I found nothing new at the spot where the weapon had been fired. Comstock was sequestered in negotiations with Broadhurst and Vinet for the entire day. The household was bustling with people, which made it impossible for me to search the Broadhursts' rooms again. I occupied myself with re-reading Frank's report, spinning theory after theory to account for the slim set of facts we had. I felt more muddled than before.

As evening approached, the ladies retired to their rooms to dress for the dance. Soon after, I saw the men leaving Comstock's library to do the same. Judging by the wide grins of Vinet and Broadhurst, the negotiations had obviously been successful, though Comstock's distracted air suggested that not everyone was pleased with the outcome. He avoided my eye and headed straight for his rooms.

There was still no sign of Leonard Frasier. With a heavy heart I realized the time had come to send a message to Frank. I scribbled a quick note. *Frasier may be the one responsible after all. Keep a watch for him. Will explain later.*

I hurried down to the kitchen, where a lone cook's assistant was putting away pots. "Is there anyone who can run a message to Mr. Wynch at the dance hall?"

The maid puckered her brow at the urgency in my tone. "Well, miss, e'ryone's busy jes' now." Her brow cleared. "I 'spect one of the stable boys could do it." She jerked a thumb toward the back door. I thanked her and hurried out.

Once that was accomplished and I was twenty-five cents the poorer for it, I realized that Sally and Enid were expecting me to help them get ready.

I pasted on a smile before entering Sally's room. "My, don't you two look lovely," I said.

Indeed, the young ladies were the picture of demure debutantes, each dressed in a froth of white, with a dash of pale accent color, hair piled high in an elaborate coiffeur, coquettish fan at the ready.

Enid and Sally beamed at me, each other, and their reflections in the glass.

"Miss Hamilton, would you help me choose a brooch?" Enid asked. She pointed to the Louis XIV armoire. "In the case over there."

I picked up a black lacquer case inlaid with mother-of-pearl and coral. "What a splendid box."

Enid nodded. "Isn't it? Father gave it to me just before we came to visit."

I opened the lid. The interior was lined in a sumptuous peach velvet and filled with both jewelry and girlhood keepsakes. I picked up a humble piece of rose quartz and raised an eyebrow in mock severity. "You collect rocks in your jewel case, Miss Broadhurst?" The girls giggled.

"The brooches are at the bottom," Enid prompted. "Which do you think I should wear tonight? I thought perhaps the aquamarine."

I set aside the top tray and carried the open box over to the dressing table, my thumb along the inside and my fingers curled around the outside. I paused.

There was a half-inch gap between the bottom interior and the exterior of the box. I felt around again with my thumb. I was sure of it.

My heart beat faster. Michael Broadhurst had given his daughter this case. What better place to hide something than among his daughter's possessions?

I didn't dare look at the box more closely now. It would have to wait until I was alone in the house.

CHAPTER 8

*A*t last, the family and guests had climbed into their carriages and the house was quiet.

I waited now for the staff to depart, sifting through Comstock's notes in the library, as was expected of the diligent Miss Hamilton. Finally, Elise tapped on the partly open door. "Miss? We're leaving now. Will you be all right by yourself?"

I nodded.

"There's a dinner tray for you in the kitchen, keeping warm."

"Thank you, Elise."

As soon as I heard the front door close, I hurried up the main staircase to Sally's room. My heart pounded. Please heaven that whatever was hidden in Enid's jewel case would solve this mystery and clear Leonard of suspicion. With a chill in the pit of my stomach, I realized I still had feelings for the man.

Enid had left her case in Sally's room. Careful to hold it so that the contents wouldn't be disturbed, I probed along the velvet lining, the bottom, and the sides. There had to be some sort of spring or pull to open the recess, though not something that could be triggered by careless handling.

I found it at last, a sliding panel where the back met the hinges.

An envelope was wedged in the gap. It contained several sheets of paper, along with a smaller slip, which was faded and barely legible. I set it aside and read the other pages.

It was fortunate that no one was in the house. I was soon completely absorbed in what turned out to be a report on the past life of Henry Altree Comstock. I hadn't even finished reading before I understood why Comstock had acceded to Broadhurst's disproportionate division of profits from Vinet's invention. He had no choice.

To gain an edge in his partnership with Comstock, Broadhurst had turned to the tool which had served him most effectively in the past. Blackmail.

Comstock might be considered a pillar of society and the salvation of Rose Glen, but he had been less than upstanding decades earlier. According to the report, Comstock had bought defective carbines on the cheap during the war, re-tooled them, and sold them to the War Department for a huge profit. The problem was he had not refurbished them all to work properly. Some were only cosmetically polished to look that way. Whether he was lazy, cheap, or in a hurry—there was a tremendous demand for munitions back in those days—the end result was the same. Comstock's defective carbines made their way to the 1st U.S. Cavalry regiment and had either jammed or exploded in men's faces.

Reading further down the report, I saw why Comstock had not been brought up later on charges. The bill of sale for those particular carbines could not be found in the Army's records. All they had to go on was the name stenciled on the crates—Ambrose Fletcher, another munitions merchant who, like Comstock, kept a warehouse near the Boston rail yard. Fletcher strenuously denied having anything to do with the carbines, though he could not account for how his crates had come to be used. His foreman, in charge of such matters at the time, had been killed in the later years of the war. With so little evidence, the matter was dropped.

A few months after the inquiry was closed, Fletcher was found in his warehouse, dead by a single rifle shot. The killer had never been found.

I felt a chill of recognition as I read that part. The connections were becoming clearer. I read on.

Broadhurst's investigator had been thorough. Upon learning that Fletcher's warehouse foreman and Comstock had been on friendly terms back in those days, the investigator searched among what remained of the foreman's effects and found the bill of sale for Fletcher's crates. Comstock had indeed bought the crates, having run short of his own. The date coincided with the time frame in which the carbines were shipped. I looked at the smaller slip of paper. Despite the faded ink, I could see it was a receipt.

Flimsy evidence, to be sure, should the federal government wish to prosecute Comstock more than twenty years after the fact. However, it was more than enough to tarnish Comstock's good name and his debutante daughter's social prospects. Broadhurst wielded a potent weapon. And Comstock, fearful that Frank and I would learn his secret, had called off the investigation.

None of this illuminated the mysteries of the mill sabotage and the murder attempts, however. It was obvious Broadhurst was not to blame for those. He'd get no money from an extortion victim who was penniless—or dead. Someone else was responsible. But who?

Wait, there *was* a connection. The report had said the defective carbines had been supplied to the 1st U.S. Cavalry regiment. But during what action? I looked at the report more closely.

Comstock's defective carbines made their way to the 1st U.S. Cavalry, engaged in the Chancellorsville Campaign.

Now it all made sense.

$\sim$

I have come to understand that solving a case is not always a plodding trek from clue to clue or day-to-day surveillance of a suspect. Sometimes, the solution comes as an intuitive flash, where all of the pieces that one did not even realize were being assembled become whole in an instant. This was one of those moments. I knew who was responsible for the sabotage and the attempts on Comstock's life, and I knew why.

Simon Dwyer was our man.

Dwyer and his son Connor had been in the 1st Massachusetts Cavalry during the war. Dwyer was wounded and Connor killed during Stoneman's Raid, a major cavalry action of the Chancellorsville Campaign. I didn't know the circumstances of the young man's death, but it was too much of a coincidence that Comstock's defective carbines had been there, too.

Simon Dwyer, nursing a more terrible wound than the one in his leg. He had lost his son, "the light of his life," as Comstock had put it. Had Dwyer killed Ambrose Fletcher, the man originally blamed for the bad carbines? I was sure of it.

Simon Dwyer, the indispensable head machinist, both at the mill and in the Comstock home. How easy it would be for him to come upon Leonard's tie clasp—no doubt left carelessly somewhere in the house—and drop it beside the loom he'd sabotaged. Comstock said that Dwyer and the townspeople had a mutual care for each other. Dwyer wouldn't want the mill workers to lose their livelihoods. None of the factory incidents had created irreparable damage. It need only be damaging enough to distract from the real purpose.

Which was what? Comstock's death? That's what we'd all assumed, but it couldn't be. The death of Henry Altree Comstock would decimate the town's livelihood just as surely as a fire or other catastrophe. Dwyer knew that. As an intimate of the household, he would be aware that Comstock's son Gerard felt no obligation toward the mill or the town. The son would sell it to one such as Broadhurst, who would pick it clean of its useful parts and move on.

No, Dwyer didn't want that. What he wanted was far more devastating to his enemy.

Without stopping to reassemble the jewel case, I snatched my coat from the hall and ran to the stables. I needed a means to get to the cotillion, quickly.

CHAPTER 9

*R*attling along in a farm cart did not allow for conversation with the sulky gardener, who obviously thought me demented for rousting him out of bed to rush me to the dance hall. As I clutched the sides of the seat to keep from being tossed off my perch, I thought back over it again, testing my theory from every angle.

The incidents had begun last week. The Broadhursts had visited the Comstocks a week before that. Going by the date of the report, Broadhurst had learned Comstock's secret during that visit. Had he told Dwyer? Everyone in the area was familiar with Dwyer's sad history. Perhaps Broadhurst wanted to sway the man's allegiance. Or Dwyer could have overheard a conversation between Broadhurst and the investigator who had submitted the report, or perhaps between Broadhurst and his wife.

The sabotage had been selective. The fire, quickly controlled, and the damaged loom, which Dwyer would be asked to repair. The explosion had come next. A machinist would have little difficulty rigging a bomb to explode at the opening of the office door. Dwyer knew Comstock was away on business. He also knew that Gerard would be working in his father's office that day.

Dwyer wanted to kill Gerard. And he wanted Comstock alive, to suffer.

No doubt Dwyer considered it fitting. A son for a son.

But the plan had not gone smoothly. Dwyer had left several innocents in his vengeful wake. Ambrose Fletcher, years ago. The messenger boy, just last week. I wondered if Dwyer felt any remorse about that.

I thought about Dwyer's most recent attempt—the single shot as the house party returned from the concert. Again, the plans were known in advance. There was plenty of time, even for a man with a severe limp, to reconnoiter the area and set up a favorable location. His cavalry service had proved him to be an accomplished horseman. But why shoot Frank? Was it too dark for Dwyer to see his target clearly, or did he want to get Frank out of the way in order to kill Gerard later, perhaps in a more spectacular manner?

A public, festive event such as a debutante cotillion would serve the purpose.

I looked at the driver. "Are we almost there?" I shouted, over the clatter of wheels.

"Another mile, miss!" the gardener shouted back.

I fumed at the delay. Here I had warned Frank about Leonard Frasier, while the kindly, helpful Simon Dwyer would be allowed to slip in, claim something was in need of repair, and no one would give him a second glance. I gave a passing thought to Leonard, wondering what could have called him away from this morning's meeting. Perhaps he was at the dance tonight and had changed into his evening attire elsewhere. If so, Frank would have him unjustly detained, and both men would be ready to spit nails when I arrived.

As we pulled up to the hall, I jumped off the cart without waiting for assistance and ran to find Frank.

Every light was blazing in the dance hall windows, casting flickering shadows on the frozen ground. I shaded my eyes and glanced along the side wall of the building. Two men in serving uniform stood in the shadows, heads together in quiet conversation. Were they part of Frank's security team or servants? That was the drawback to assuming a disguise. Your own people may not recognize you.

They looked up as I approached. I had to be careful not to give anything away.

"Has either of you seen Frank Wynch?" I asked, still huffing from my dash across the lawn.

The men gave me blank looks. Definitely not Pinkertons.

"His arm is in a sling," I added.

One of them pointed toward the rear of the building. "Kitchen entrance, last I saw him."

I nodded my thanks and scurried in that direction, heedless of the chill seeping through my shoes.

I finally found Frank outside the French doors to the billiard room, keeping an eye on Comstock discreetly through the glass. His face brightened at the sight of me. He gestured for me to join him in the gazebo a few yards away, still within sight of his charge, but out of earshot.

"I got your note. No sign of Frasier," Frank said. "What's this all about anyway?"

My heart sank. Where was Leonard? But I couldn't worry about him now. "Have you seen Simon Dwyer?"

Frank started in surprise. "The machinist from the mill? No. Why would he be here? Nothing has broken down that I know of."

I pulled out the report on Comstock and thrust it at Frank. "I found this hidden away in Enid Broadhurst's jewel case. Simon Dwyer is the one we want, not Leonard Frasier. I suspect Dwyer's planning something for tonight."

Frank frowned over the paper in the dim light. "I can't make this out. Why don't you save us some time and tell me what's in here."

I quickly summarized the contents, along with my conclusions

65

about Dwyer. I was just about to tell him of Dwyer's true intention to kill Gerard when Frank interrupted.

"If Dwyer's our man, why did I get a note from you only two hours ago that named Leonard Frasier as the one to watch for?" His eyes narrowed in suspicion. "I noticed you and Frasier were quite...cozy...last night. You were even wearing his jacket. You're holding something back from me, and I have a feeling I'm not going to like it."

A hot flush crept up my neck and cheeks. "We were not *cozy*. It was nothing like that. But we did have a relationship, years ago. Before I met you."

"And you didn't think it important to tell me sooner? You've jeopardized the entire operation," Frank hissed between clenched teeth.

I glanced down at my fists before meeting his eyes. "I wanted this case so badly. I know I should have told you. But Leonard isn't responsible for any of the incidents. Dwyer is making it look that way. Can't you see? The report about Comstock, right there in your hand...it clearly points to Dwyer's motive. And you *know* he had the opportunity."

"Then why did you tell me Frasier was to blame? You ladies are so fickle," Frank sneered. "Did you and Frasier have a falling-out, and then you decided to make trouble for him? Or do you regret telling me the truth and are trying to cover up for him now?"

"Listen to yourself," I snapped. "I can remember many an occasion when you suspected the wrong man. Did I ever call you fickle? Stop acting the jealous husband. It ill suits you. No matter who I suspected before, this"—I tapped the report—"changes everything. And I'll tell you something else: you'd better guard the son, because he's Dwyer's true target. *Not* H.A. Comstock."

Frank's mouth hung open.

I took a few steps back, looking up at the roofline. "Where is Gerard now?"

"In the ballroom. What are you doing?"

I made a *shushing* gesture as I craned my neck for a better look. "I thought I saw movement." I pointed to a balcony above the garden. "Over there. Does that lead into the ballroom?"

Frank nodded, squinting in the dark. "It opens onto the upper gallery. But I don't see anyone up there. Your eyes are playing tricks on you, Pen."

I saw nothing now, but I was sure I had a moment ago.

"We already locked those doors as a precaution and roped off the gallery staircase," Frank added. "Anyway, how could he have gotten up there with that leg of his?"

I didn't bother to answer. A simple lock and a bad leg wouldn't stop Dwyer. "Get your men over to the nearby roof—*quietly*. And for heaven's sake, tell them not to shoot unless they have to." I left him before he had a chance to object.

I edged along the perimeter of the house toward the front entrance. *How did Dwyer reach the balcony?* I saw no ladder, and he certainly could not have climbed any of the trees and swung onto the parapet, though perhaps a more active man could manage it. Dwyer must have reached the balcony from the inside.

I heard the strains of a quadrille starting up as I reached the front steps. I glanced down ruefully at my somber navy wool skirt and pinstripe shirtwaist, not at all appropriate for an elegant evening affair. I wrapped my shawl about me more closely. Perhaps I could slip in unobtrusively.

But Frank's arrangements had been thorough, and one of his hired men stopped me as soon as I gained the front hall.

"Here now, who are you, and where are you going in such a hurry?" he demanded. He waved over another operative from the far side of the room while keeping a painful grip on my arm.

"I'm Mrs. Wynch, Frank's wife." I gestured toward the open doors of the ballroom. A portion of the gallery was visible from this angle, but no sign of Dwyer. "We believe a sniper has gotten past you."

Both men stared at me as if I'd claimed to be Queen Victoria. "*No one* has gotten past *us*, including you, young lady," one said.

"Take your hands off me," I snarled, leaning in. My height put me nose to nose with the man clutching my arm. Startled, he let go and took an involuntary step back.

"There's no time for this," I snapped, rubbing my arm. The brute. "You must take Simon Dwyer into custody before he kills Gerard Comstock. Quickly, follow me."

"Simon?" The men looked at each other doubtfully. I realized with a sinking heart that Frank had hired local men for tonight's job, and here I was, telling them to capture a beloved old man.

This was taking too much time. Well, there was more than one way to get them to follow me.

I bolted through the ballroom doors before they could grab me again, weaving between clusters of quadrille dancers—no doubt causing many a young debutante to lose count of her steps in the round—as I located the stairway leading to the upper gallery. The shouts were close behind.

I ducked past the last dancer in my path and under the velveteen rope strung across the bottom stair. I took the steps two at a time, holding my skirts high in both hands to keep from tripping. Even so, I caught my heel a couple of times and nearly fell backward. I could hear the pounding footfalls and heavy breathing just a few steps behind. My legs felt like lead, but I kept going. I finally reached the gallery.

At first, I saw no one through any of the balcony windows. The bright chandeliers of the ballroom illuminated only my own gasping reflection.

Then I noticed a balcony window on the far side had been opened a crack. I sucked in a breath. A rifle barrel protruded through the opening. It was aimed between the gallery railings, pointed downward at the crowd. I watched the barrel alter direction. It now pointed at *me*.

The Pinkerton men had caught up, but they froze, staring at the scene. No help from that quarter.

When one cannot retreat, it's time to advance, Father used to say.

"Simon, *stop!*" I shouted, running toward the barrel—or, more precisely, toward the man behind it. I could see him through the glass as I approached. He had pulled back from the sights, gaping at the spectacle of a woman charging at him.

I pushed hard at the glass door, which swung outward and caught him in the chest. As he lost his balance, his finger fumbled for the trigger. I flinched.

A shadow behind Dwyer jumped from the balcony railing and tackled him. Frank's outside guards had caught up at last.

But the man hauling Dwyer to his feet wasn't a Pinkerton.

"L-Leonard?" I stammered in astonishment. "What are you... where have you...?"

Leonard Frasier stepped out of the dim balcony into the light of the gallery. He wearily passed a thrashing Simon Dwyer over to the two Pinkerton men as Frank came running up the gallery stairs.

"What happened to you?" I exclaimed. Leonard was a bedraggled mess: clothes muddy and torn, scalp dried with crusted blood, a welt puffing up one eye.

He grimaced and jerked his head toward Dwyer. "This one sent me a note this morning, saying he knew who was behind the sabotage and murder attempts. He said he'd found important evidence at the boat house and asked me to meet him there."

By this point, Frank had caught up to us, huffing from exertion.

"Then what?" I asked.

Leonard looked rueful. "I'm embarrassed to admit he caught me completely off guard. Knocked me out. I awoke facedown in a rowboat at the boat house, trussed up like a Christmas goose."

Dwyer continued to struggle in the arms of his captors.

Frank stepped outside to the balcony and returned with Dwyer's weapon. He looked it over appreciatively. "Just as I thought—a Spencer carbine. They started issuing these to cavalry regiments in late 1863."

Not interested in Frank's lesson in old weaponry, I turned back to Leonard. "How did you escape?"

Leonard self-consciously straightened his collar and cuffs. "I'll tell you the rest later." He gestured toward the crowd of murmuring cotillion guests below. All faces were turned up at us.

Heavens, I'd completely forgotten about them. I looked down and saw the pale faces of Henry and Gerard Comstock, who couldn't take their eyes from the gun in Frank's hand. Sally and Enid were close behind, clutching one another.

Leonard turned to Frank and whispered, "You don't want to bring Dwyer through that crowd downstairs. There's a ladies' lounge over there." He pointed to a small paneled door near the gallery stairs. "You can take him out through the kitchen when the police get here."

Frank gave Leonard a grateful look, then cleared his throat to address the guests. "Ladies and gentlemen, please pardon the interruption. Nothing to worry about. Everything is well in hand." He locked eyes with Comstock. "Sir?" He inclined his head toward the lounge door. H.A. Comstock, his son Gerard close at his heels, hurried up to join us.

The ladies' lounge seemed an incongruous place for such a meeting, with its delicately turned chairs, swathes of gold-velvet window hangings, and dried flower arrangements that littered nearly every table at hand. There was no help for it, of course.

An ashen-faced Simon Dwyer sat on the divan, flanked by two

of Frank's men. By this point he had stopped squirming and sat quietly, though his eyes blazed as he watched Comstock conferring with Frank and Leonard in the far corner of the room. I saw Frank pass over the report I had found in Enid's jewel box. When Frank thought no one was looking, he awkwardly adjusted his sling and flexed his fingers.

I was sitting close by the fire, though I still felt cold. A subdued Gerard Comstock sat beside me. From my position, I could see Comstock glance over the report, with Leonard shamelessly reading over his shoulder, eyes widening. They conferred in low voices, glancing my way several times.

Finally, the three rejoined the rest of us. Comstock put a hand on Leonard's shoulder and guided him to a bench. "Sit. You look ready to fall over. Wynch has sent someone for the doctor as well as the police." His eyes softened. "I owe you a great debt, my friend."

Then Comstock looked over at me, lips twitching—no doubt at the sight of my disheveled hair, rumpled blouse, and the dragging hem I'd caught on the stairs. "Miss Hamilton, I owe you a debt of gratitude as well. I must admit I had my doubts when Wynch first proposed bringing you in on this matter. But you astonish me, young lady."

I smiled.

Frank touched Comstock on the arm and looked inquiringly at his son.

Comstock sighed. "Gerard, I would ask that you step out of the room. There are personal matters to discuss that do not concern you."

I raised an eyebrow. Even now, Comstock was attempting to keep his secret from his son?

Gerard turned an angry red. "It very much concerns me, Father, and you know it." He touched the healing wound on his temple.

Simon Dwyer spoke for the first time. "Your sonny's right. But you don't want him to know about the deaths and misery you caused, do you?" He gave a bitter laugh. "Tryin' to spare your own son, but you didn't spare mine!" His voice broke. "Connor was my all. You took him from me." He put his head in his hands and sobbed.

"Is this true?" Gerard asked his father, eyes wide.

A pained look crossed Comstock's face. "I never knew before now. I had no intention of hurting anyone. It was long ago. Before you were born."

"It has to do with the carbines your father refurbished for the Army during the war," I added, noting Gerard's confused expression. I turned to Comstock. "Your son deserves to know. The time for excuses has long passed."

Comstock rubbed a hand across the back of his neck. "I admit, I was ambitious. I wanted to prove I didn't need my father's wealth to succeed, that I could run my own business. I suppose I took on an order I had no hope of completing. But what was I to do?" Comstock turned to his son with pleading eyes. "Shortcuts were necessary."

"So you shipped weapons that you knew wouldn't work," Leonard said sharply.

Comstock sighed and looked out the dark window.

"What happened then?" Gerard's face had grown pale.

When it was obvious that Comstock had retreated into his own thoughts, I took up the story. "Your father's malfunctioning guns reached the 1st Massachusetts Cavalry. That was the regiment Mr. Dwyer and his son served in. Connor was killed and his father wounded during the Chancellorsville Campaign." I looked over at Simon Dwyer, head still in his hands. I softened my voice. "Mr. Dwyer, what exactly happened on Stoneman's Raid? I assume the weapons were to blame?"

Dwyer lifted his head to look at me. "They were. We'd just surprised a picket of Rebs an' were trying to return fire. My gun jammed. Connor's blew up in his face. I saw him collapse upon his horse. I got hit when I rode over to help him." He shook his head. "But there was no help left on earth for my boy. I've spent the rest of my life wishing the Reb's bullet had hit me in the heart instead of the leg."

"When the Army's investigation of the defective carbines pointed to Ambrose Fletcher, you decided to assassinate him," I said. "Until a couple of weeks ago, you thought you had avenged your son."

Dwyer gave a miserable nod.

"How did you learn Mr. Comstock was to blame?" I asked.

Dwyer sighed. "I overheard Broadhurst, last time he was here. I was at the house, in the laundry room, jes' about to work on the clothes wringer. He was talking with a man outside. They didn' know I was there. When I heard 'war' and 'carbines,' I slipped under the window to listen."

Frank broke in. "You are responsible, then, for the incidents at the factory—the fire, the damaged power loom, the bomb? And the bomb was intended to kill Gerard, not his father?"

Dwyer gave a brief nod.

"Why go to such elaborate means? Why not simply shoot Comstock's son when you first learned the truth?" I asked. Gerard winced.

Dwyer folded his arms and glared.

Frank looked up from his notes. "If you cooperate, Mr. Dwyer, they may go easier on you. We'll know everything eventually. Come now, this is the chance to tell us the rest of your story."

We waited.

Dwyer sighed. "I suppose I'm done for, no matter what. Well then. I thought if it looked like there was sabotage before Comstock's son was killed by the bomb, folks would blame the mill's biggest rival, Broadhurst, for all of it. First I made sure there'd be no lasting damage to the factory. I don't want the town to lose its living."

"That's also why you didn't kill Comstock," I said.

Dwyer gave a bitter nod. "Then I learned that he and Broad-hurst were going into partnership for a patent, so it didn't make sense anymore to blame Broadhurst. I decided to shift the blame to Mr. Frasier. I'd heard Comstock talking with his lawyer about writing a will in Mr. Frasier's favor."

"So you left my tie clasp at the power loom after you wrecked it," Leonard chimed in angrily, "and lured me to the boat house today. Why did you attack me?"

Dwyer hesitated.

"I think he planned a suicide for you, Mr. Frasier," I said, when it was obvious that Dwyer didn't care to admit to a second attempted murder. "By leaving you unconscious and tied up in a rowboat, it would be a simple matter, later on, to row out to the middle of the river, tie a weight to your legs, unbind your hands, and throw you over. Perhaps the boat would be left adrift, with a note inside, admitting to shooting Gerard so that Comstock would leave the mill to you in his will. Something about having a change of heart and no longer being able live with yourself. The blow to your head would be attributed to rocks along the bottom of the river."

Dwyer gave me an uneasy glance.

"But why wait until later?" Frank asked.

"My guess is he didn't want to risk Leonard's body being found in the river too soon, *before* the cotillion. The current is quite strong this time of year." I glanced ruefully in Leonard's direction. Undoubtedly, other ladies of his acquaintance would not speak so casually of the disposition of his corpse.

"What I don't understand is how he expected to get away after shooting Gerard tonight," Frank said.

"I can answer that," Leonard said. "There's a ladder up on the balcony, propped out of sight. He must have pulled it up after him, to avoid attracting the attention of your security men. Then he'd simply reverse the process. Once he escaped, it wouldn't matter if the ladder was found."

Frank unconsciously adjusted his sling again and looked at Dwyer. "Why change tactics and switch to using the carbine?" He picked up the weapon and looked it over again. "Were you issued this in the cavalry?"

Dwyer nodded. "Later on, after Stoneman's Raid, we got brand-new Spencers. To replace the worthless carbines most of us had." The look of pure loathing directed at Comstock was wasted, as that man kept his gaze fixed upon the window. Was Comstock embarrassed, distracted, or bored with the proceedings? I couldn't tell.

"But why shoot *me* last night?" Frank asked Dwyer.

"I have no quarrel with you, even if you are helping *him*." Dwyer jerked a thumb toward Comstock. "I only wanted you out of my way tonight. I had quite the spectacle planned. A dance they would never forget."

I shivered at Dwyer's twisted smile.

"Besides," Dwyer went on, "I made sure you were only wounded. Believe me, if I'd wanted you dead, you would be."

Fist clenched, Frank stood. I quickly jumped up and put a hand on his arm.

The moment passed, and Frank regained his composure. "You never answered my original question," he said, voice level. "Why switch to using the carbine as the means to kill Gerard?"

Dwyer shifted on the divan. Frank's men tensed, poised to grab him should he attempt to rise. But he merely passed a hand over his face. His eyes had grown misty, and his lips trembled. I could see it was a struggle for the old man to keep his emotions under control.

"Two people died at my hand that should not," Dwyer said at last. "Fletcher, and then that boy. By using my carbine, I could make sure I didn't kill another innocent."

"Except for your plans to kill *me*," Leonard said caustically.

Comstock had come out of his reverie at last, his face an angry, mottled red. "*My son* is innocent, damn you!" He charged at Dwyer. Frank and Leonard stepped in to restrain him.

Dwyer didn't flinch and looked Comstock square in the eye. "So was Connor."

CHAPTER 10

$\mathcal{L}$eonard Frasier escorted me to the train station the next day.

"Thank you for bringing me," I said. "Frank is busy with his report." Frank and I had already said our goodbyes, painful though they were.

Take me back, Pen. I'm a changed man.

I had changed, too.

Leonard took my bag from the hansom driver. "I'm sorry to see you go."

I nodded.

"I do wish you'd stay," he added.

We climbed the steps to the platform. "There's nothing to be gained by my staying," I said quietly. I met his eyes. "We both know that."

He shrugged, reluctant to agree, but I knew he recognized the reality of it. Estranged or not, I was married to Frank Wynch, and that was that.

"Besides, I have responsibilities back home," I said.

Solving the case had immensely improved my prospects in that regard. A nice cash bonus—given by a subdued but grateful

H.A. Comstock for saving his son—was secreted in an inner skirt pocket, along with a glowing letter of reference that I would present to William Pinkerton. Frank had been true to his promise at last. Between the letter and Frank's final report, I hoped to soon be employing my lockpicks rather than my china-painting brushes.

"May I write you, at least?" Leonard asked.

"I hope you will," I said brightly, "although you may be much too busy."

Leonard had been put in charge of mill operations indefinitely. The Comstocks were leaving town for an extended stay with the Vinets in New Orleans, although father and son would return for Dwyer's trial. The publicity would be ugly. However, if Comstock handled the situation with penitence and generous reparations to the war widows' fund, he and his family should survive the scandal. But that was up to Comstock.

That reminded me of something else. "Leonard, did I hear correctly that Comstock plans to confront Broadhurst about his blackmail scheme and nullify the patent agreement?"

Leonard smiled. "H.A. realized he had nothing to lose, now that his secret was out. He's already done it. This morning, he went to Vinet first and confessed all, then told him what Broadhurst had done."

"How did Vinet take it?" I asked. Considering Madame Vinet's earlier comment—*il a un secret*—Vinet must have known something was amiss.

"Well, the French don't shock as easily as we Americans when it comes to scandal," Leonard winked. "He was sympathetic to Comstock's predicament and reluctant to have business dealings with an underhanded fellow such as Broadhurst. So they confronted him together and got him to nullify the partnership."

"How did they manage that?"

"They gave Broadhurst a choice. Void the agreement quietly,

or be arrested for blackmail, whereby the agreement would be nullified by the courts."

"So Comstock won't be getting Vinet's patent, after all," I said. I felt sorry for the Vinets, remembering Madame's excitement that her husband's hard work had finally come to fruition.

"Not so fast," Leonard said with a grin. "I am the new partner in the patent agreement."

"*You?*" I said, incredulous.

"Comstock had that same look on his face when I told him I had more than enough funds to cover Broadhurst's share."

"Speaking of money," I asked, "do we know why Broadhurst had all that cash in his briefcase?"

Leonard frowned. "Apparently, he had promised a bonus to the investigator who uncovered H.A.'s secret. If he was able to successfully use it against Comstock, he was to pay the detective an additional five hundred dollars."

I sighed. Such men, profiting from fear and threats, soil the reputation of detectives everywhere. It was a lesson I was to be reminded of in years to come.

The thunderous vibration beneath our feet warned us of the approaching train. "I don't know if I'll see you again," I said. I blinked rapidly as my eyes prickled. *Mercy*, it must be the coal dust. Even modern train travel was not devoid of nuisances.

He took my hand in his. "Who knows? I may need to travel to Chicago for business."

I gave a wan smile. "Or perhaps an assignment of mine will bring me back here."

The conductor paced the platform. We felt the *whoosh* of air as the train pulled into the station. "All aboard the express to Chicago!"

Leonard gripped my hand more tightly. "Let us promise, then, that this isn't goodbye."

Not trusting myself to speak, I nodded.

Once aboard the crowded car, I secured a seat beside a young lady of perhaps twenty. As I settled in, she set aside the journal she had been writing in and smoothed her skirts. "Where are you going?" she asked politely.

"Chicago. And you?"

She grimaced. "I have much farther to go."

I smiled. *So do I.*

~

THE END

AFTERWORD

I hope you enjoyed the story. Please consider leaving a quick review at your favorite online venue. A single sentence as to whether or not you liked it, along with clicking on the star rating you see fit, can go a long way. Ratings create a digital "word of mouth" that help readers find books they will love, particularly those written by independently published authors. Thank you!

The next Penelope Hamilton story, "The Mystery of Schroon Lake Inn," is available now!

Missing jewels...a haunted inn...a long-held secret...

Penelope Hamilton Wynch, one of the few female operatives employed at the Pinkerton Agency in 1886, is sent to the Adirondacks to investigate the mysterious happenings at Schroon Lake Inn, newly renovated to cater to New York City's upper crust on summer holiday. Rumors of ghosts are bad enough, but when expensive jewelry disappears, the owner's livelihood is at stake. A woman's touch is needed.

Pen's boss, William Pinkerton, thinks he has given her the perfect cover. She is to play the part of an eccentric spirit medium, eager to experience the purported ghostly manifestations.

Unfortunately, her cover will not remain intact for long, and there are those behind the scenes who are desperate to keep the secrets of Schroon Lake Inn from coming to light. Will Pen's discoveries prove fatal? She would have to be truly clairvoyant to know....

DON'T MISS ANY OF K.B.'S RELEASES! SIGN UP HERE.

ACKNOWLEDGMENTS

It's a great time to be a historical author, with the wealth of digitized historical material available on the world wide web. For anyone interested in the background research that went into the writing of this book, I've shared some wonderful primary and secondary sources on my website, kbowenmysteries.com. I'd love to see you there.

Even in our internet age, however, a writer needs to turn to real people—for facts, advice, or moral support. This page is to thank those people. Some of these were experts, but any errors are mine alone.

To Peter Owen, who helped with Civil War battle information and weaponry.

To graphic artist Melinda VanLone, who created such a beautiful cover. She can be reached at BookCoverCorner.com.

To Kristen Lamb and the generous community of fellow writers known as WANAs, who provided advice and support. We are truly not alone.

To my mom, Ag Belin, who cheers me on in all my endeavors.

But most of all, I want to thank Paul, my partner and my love. This would not have been possible without you.

K.B. Owen
  March 2015

THE CONCORDIA WELLS MYSTERIES

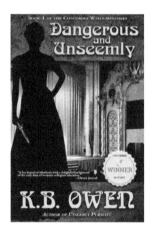

*S*et in a fictitious 1890s women's college, this cozy-style series features Miss Concordia Wells, a young lady professor who cannot resist a little unseemly sleuthing when those she cares about are at risk. Who knew higher education could be...murder?

Start with:

*Dangerous and Unseemly, book 1. Winner of **Library Journal's** "Best Mystery of 2015: SELF-e"!*

"A fun historical whodunit with a delightful background of the early days of women's collegiate education." *~Library Journal*

ALSO BY K.B. OWEN

ABOUT THE AUTHOR

K.B. Owen taught college English at universities in Connecticut and Washington, DC and holds a doctorate in 19th century British literature. A long-time mystery lover, she drew upon her teaching experiences in creating her amateur sleuth, Professor Concordia Wells and from there, lady Pinkerton Penelope Hamilton was born.

kbowenmysteries.com
contact@kbowenmysteries.com

Made in United States
North Haven, CT
02 December 2022

27640411R00055